Francis B. Nyamnjoh
Stories from Abakwa
Mind Searching
The Disillusioned African
The Convert
Souls Forgotten
Married But Available

Dibussi Tande
No Turning Back. Poems of Freedom 1990-1993

Kangsen Feka Wakai
Fragmented Melodies

Ntemfac Ofege
Namondo. Child of the Water Spirits
Hot Water for the Famous Seven
The Return of Omar
Growing Up
Children of Bethel Street

Emmanuel Fru Doh
Not Yet Damascus
The Fire Within
Africa's Political Wastelands: The Bastardization
of Cameroon

Thomas Jing
Tale of an African Woman

Peter Wuteh Vakunta
Grassfields Stories from Cameroon
Green Rape: Poetry for the Environment
Majunga Tok: Poems in Pidgin English
Cry, My Beloved Africa

Ba'bila Mutia
Coils of Mortal Flesh

Kehbuma Langmia
Titabet and the Takumbeng

Victor Elame Musinga
The Barn
The Tragedy of Mr. No Balance

Ngessimo Mathe Mutaka
Building Capacity: Using TEFL and African
Languages as Development-oriented Literacy
Tools

Milton Krieger
Cameroon's Social Democratic Front: Its History
and Prospects as an Opposition Political Party,
1990-2011

Sammy Oke Akombi
The Raped Amulet

The Woman Who Ate Python
Beware the Drives: Book of Verse

Susan Nkwentie Nde
Precipice

Francis B. Nyamnjoh &
Richard Fonteh Akum
The Cameroon GCE Crisis: A Test of
Anglophone Solidarity

Joyce Ashuntantang & Dibussi Tande
Their Champagne Party Will End! Poems in
Honor of Bate Besong

Emmanuel Achu
Disturbing the Peace

Rosemary Ekosso
The House of Falling Women

Peterkins Manyong
God the Politician

George Ngwane
The Power in the Writer: Collected Essays on
Culture, Democracy & Development in Africa

John Percival
The 1961 Cameroon Plebiscite: Choice or Betrayal

Albert Azeyeh
Réussite scolaire, faillite sociale : généalogie
mentale de la crise de l'Afrique noire francophone

Aloysius Ajab Amin & Jean-Luc Dubois
Croissance et developpement au Cameroun :
d'une croissance équilibrée à un développement
équitable

Carlson Anyangwe
Imperialistic Politics in Cameroun:
Resistance & the Inception of the Restoration of
the Statehood of Southern Cameroons

Excel Tse Chinepoh & Ntemfac A.N. Ofege
The Adventures of Chimangwe

Bill F. Ndi
K'Cracy, Trees in the Storm and Other Poems

Kathryn Toure, Therese Mungah
Shalo Tchombe & Thierry Karsenti
ICT and Changing Mindsets in Education

Alobwed'Epie
The Day God Blinked

T0198538

The Day God Blinked

Alobwed'Epie

Langaa Research & Publishing CIG
Mankon, Bamenda

Publisher:
Langaa RPCIG
(*Langaa* Research & Publishing Common Initiative Group)
P.O. Box 902 Mankon
Bamenda
North West Province
Cameroon
Langaagrp@gmail.com
www.langaapublisher.com

Distributed outside N. America by African Books Collective
orders@africanbookscollective.com
www.africanbookscollective.com

Distributed in N. America by Michigan State University Press
msupress@msu.edu
www.msupress.msu.edu

ISBN:9956-558-86-9

DISCLAIMER

This is a work of fiction. Names, characters, places, and incidents are either the author's invention or they are used fictitiously. Any resemblance to actual places and persons, living or dead, events, or locales is coincidental.

1

On March 20th 1999, at 2.30 a.m. Dande lay in the innocence of the morning. The peace of the Lord had descended, and was descending on the chosen. It may be on the one hundred and forty four thousand, or by some grace, on an additional ten thousand. A chilly wind blew across the municipal lake where I now stood to execute the crucial decision. My lips chattered, my nose ran as I shivered from cold. My son was still firmly tied on my back. I looked up at the twinkling stars, stars that were never to twinkle at him again, and a lone tear rolled down my left cheek. In that insidious situation, tears don't count. I had taken my decision. I untied the body of my son from my back and laid it on the grass by the lake. I then spread the cloth with which I had tied him onto my back on the grass. I took the limp thing and placed it on the cloth. I then tied it firmly and braced myself for the appalling decision. I moved into the lake and as it deepened and its cold water reached above my knees, I stood. With all my might, I hauled the bundle into the lake. It thumped so loudly and echoed so far and wide that I feared the whole world had heard the echo. As I strained my eyes trying to watch it sink to the bottom, I saw several searchlights rushing towards me. Presently, a combat-ready squat of six policemen surrounded me.

"Don't shake. Surrender!" they ordered in unison.

Their order meant nothing to me. I stood still, peering through the dancing stars in the lake to see my bundle sink.

"You have thrown something into the lake," they thundered.

"Yes," I answered calmly.

"What is it? What?" the ASP asked.

"My dead child," I responded calmly.

"Your dead what? You killed your child and decided to come and throw it in the municipal lake? You want to cover up your crime?" he asked in flaming anger.

"No, Sir. The child died on his own," I responded.

"Bullshit. Is this your burial ground? You have killed your baby and chosen the heart of the night to come and throw the body in the lake. You have to retrieve it from the bottom of the lake. Jump into the lake and retrieve the body," the ASP ordered.

"I can't swim," I retorted with defiance.

"But you can kill and throw bodies into the lake. You have to retrieve that body," a junior officer shouted.

"I can't swim," I said again.

"Whether you can swim or not, you have to retrieve the body from the lake. Jump into the lake," he ordered with bloodshot eyes while fidgeting with the pistol dangling by his side.

"Push me into it officer," I supplicated.

"Jump," they ordered in unison.

"Push me into it officers. Tip me over," I cried.

As I battled it out with them, a police van pulled up.

Three frogmen jumped out of it and presently, were combing the bottom of the lake. It did not take long. They soon tugged the cold wet body of my son from the bottom of the lake and dumped it at my feet. I picked up the remains of my son and kissed them passionately. That made the police boil with anger. They unleashed a flood of insults at me. One stepped forward and kicked me under the belly with his boots. My female system convulsed. My eyes turned. As I tried to maintain my balance, eight hefty hands hauled me into the van and whisked me off to the police station.

At the police station, I was dragged out of the van and taken to an apparently drunken ASP. He eyed me sideways and pulled at his coarse greying whiskers, then belched impishly. I interpreted that as a snarl before the bite.

"Girlie," he called thoughtlessly and went dead. He remained silent for a long time, perhaps caused by alcohol induced blackout. Then he called again in a noncommittal manner.

"Girlie, what happened? Why are you brought here at this time of the night?" he asked with no sting in his question. Because he was elderly, I started feeling safe in his hands.

"My child died and I threw the body into the lake," I answered with some confidence.

"Officer, teach her how a child dies and the body is thrown into the lake," he said with such harmlessness that I thought the officer would take a piece of chalk and start lecturing me on how a child dies.

Then the heavens closed against a sinner. Although the ASP did not say officers, three hefty muscular policemen stood up to break the horse. They rained truncheons on me, not minding where they hit. I reacted rather instinctively. I curled up like a pangolin and thus surrendered my back for tattooing. My body turned crusty and so warded off pain. I did not groan nor whine. I did not plead. I just surrendered myself to the men of peace to piece me up.

That apparent defiance wreaked havoc in the ASP. He seized a truncheon and came in for the kill. He landed two solid ones on the small of my back. My spine creaked, and at last I thought my twenty six year old heart could bear it no longer. But before I screamed in defeat, the ASP ordered his men to stop. I won in defeat. They lost in victory.

"That is a cup of tea - breakfast for a witch," he said as he wiped his brows with the back of his hand.

"What is your name?" he asked while sitting down.

"Lucia," I answered in a hiccough.

"Your maiden name. Your surname," he emphasized.

"I have only one name. My father withdrew my maiden name," I responded distantly.

"Why? Because you are a bad girl. Because you are a disgrace to him and the rest of your family. Yes, because you are not worthy of being identified with him. Because you are a street girl, a murderess, an outcast, a witch. Poor father. Shame!" he insulted.

I sat quiet, although the undeserved insults made my bowels turn.

"If you don't want to answer, we shall pry the answer from your lips," he warned.

"Please Sir, I can't tell, I don't know," I said rather confusedly.

"What is your father's name?" he asked with steaming anger.

"I have no father. The one I had disowned me," I answered with a frown.

"Your mother's name?" he asked.

"I have no mother. The one I had disowned me," I responded again.

"What is your occupation?" he asked, this time with a voice more edged with bitterness.

"I have none. I, I, I, I left school, I left, since I left school, school," I stammered.

"You have none, no job, but to incubate and spread diseases, breed, murder and throw babies in lakes and so increase the work of an already battered and underpaid police force," he said contemptuously.

That venom tore through my spleen and shattered the last iota of my personality. I have always been subjected to both psychological and emotional torture but none has ever placed me at the border of contemplating suicide. I owed most of my torturers some good turn but I owed the police nothing. They had introduced physical torture on me, and now the ASP was gluing me with a mental picture of myself that I could not contain. Physical torture, especially one with truncheons disfigures the body and makes it unattractive to onlookers. But mental torture disfigures the mind and makes it unattractive to oneself. One rejects her being and opts for suicide. I opted for it at the hands of the ASP and his men and so, gave him a telling off.

"Monsieur ASP, if you say you are overworked and underpaid then you are ungrateful. The police force is the most irrelevant working force in the Republic of Ewawa. When the police are called upon to chase a thief, they abandon the chase half way and chase taxi men," I said with a trembling voice.

"Were you a taxi man when they caught you?" he asked.

"I was not, but I know when the police are called upon to investigate a crime they distort the evidence when the culprit bribes them."

"And that is why you are about to bribe us now? Do you know your crime is worse than that of a taxi man?"

"I have committed no crime. It is you who thinks I have committed a crime. I know of several cases of road accidents where the police made aggrieved persons guilty."

"So you consider yourself an aggrieved person in this case and the police have made you guilty. You better mind your p's and q's."

"I would have done so but for your claim that you are underpaid. I know the salaries of the police, gendarmes and military were never slashed. They have risk allowances. They have the leeway to do whatever they want to do to make money. They have set up clandestine tollgates all over the city and even in the most dangerous and remotest roads in the country. When they are asked to investigate corrupt Ministers and other plunderers of Ewawa economy, they distort facts and let them free."

"They let them free and arrest you?" the ASP asked with flaming scorn.

"Yes, they arrest the innocent. There is no major crime in this country to which the police are not the perpetrators or witnesses. Look at the case of the burning of the People's Congress Hall, external investigators hold that the Secretary General, a once police top brass, fearful that his looting would be discovered, planted a time bomb in the building. Your investigators blame the incident on poor electrification."

"Are you sure of your facts? You are a hardened criminal and I am afraid you can be charged of libel".

"Whether I am charged or not, the population is fed up with the police. So, don't hurt the already hurt. We know what is happening in Ewawa. There would have long been a take-over in this country if the kleptocrats had not neutralized the forces of law and order, by making them co-plunderers of Ewawa economy."

"Isn't Ewawa lucky to have patriots like you? You are going to redeem Ewawa," the ASP interjected.

"I may be incapable of redeeming Ewawa. But the fact is that people are fast realizing that something has to be done. There is too much abuse of power. The police have unlimited powers and opportunities to make money wherever and whenever they want. The mouth that eats does not talk. Does it? Only yours does. It is only in Ewawa that cane-bearing slouching law enforcement top brass lead march pasts. Each broods over heavy budgets, not minding the dangers of old age and the threat of the deprived youth. We know that Ewawa is a military state. So, don't blindfold the public," I spluttered, steaming with rage.

The office fell silent. One could hear the heartbeat of a child. The ASP and his men tended to turn a deaf ear to what I had said. I thought my washing him down had made no impact. I thought the police were too used to those types of insults and mine was simply brushed aside. That silent response to what I had thought would be suicidal filled me with fear when my anger subsided and I thought things over. Furthermore, I saw some goodness in living after all. I inwardly regretted and thought of apologizing to make good my relations with the ASP and his men. But on second thought, I decided to hold my grounds. It was getting to dawn and by the grace of God the officers would change guard. The new comers won't know what I had said and I would create a better relationship with them.

"Can you state your case, Miss Lucia?" the ASP asked with some bitterness in his voice.

"Sir, I have no case to state but to tell you that my son died and I threw the body into the lake," I said rather calmly.

"I have warned you to co-operate. Intransigence won't help you here. There is no God here," the ASP warned with betraying anger.

"Sir, I believe there is no God anywhere," I retorted rather firmly with rejuvenated embittered courage.

The ASP's eyes flashed flaming scorn at me. He pulled at his whiskers, stood up with a twang, growled, and his men charged at me. This time, they were more indiscriminate. The truncheons fell all over my body with untold savagery. I could no longer protect my face. At a certain point one of the officers held my hands and so exposed my chest. His colleague took aim at my breasts, and landed a solid blow on the right one. The pain coursed through me with the force of a thousand million watt electric current subjecting me to epileptic spasms. Before I could recover from it, one of the blows opened a gash across my forehead and let the hose loose. Blood jetted out with such force that the wall got wet. One of the hounds rushed to me with a drawn snuff-coated handkerchief and... I think I past out at that time.

Around mid-morning, I was ripped from sleep by excruciating darts of pain. I discovered I was in hospital. When I opened my eyes, the female police officer probably left behind to keep watch handed me a prescription. I was expected to buy an anti-tetanus injection, some stitching implements, some dressing and fresh wound medication including gauze and suture, and anti-inflammatory and pain-killing drugs. I read the prescription in the blur of partially closed eyelids - glued with caked blood. My pain vanished as I retched from disgust and anger.

"Officer," I called the absentminded fellow who was paying more attention to patients quarrelling with an impudent nurse who had allowed in her relative who had come late to see the Doctor.

"Officer," I called again. "Has the Doctor on duty seen this prescription?"

"He wrote it himself. He has been waiting for you to provide the drugs for him to stitch your wound. I believe it is time for him to return. His colleague has come. I think he is already handing over. So, hurry," she said emphatically.

"Officer, are you sure the Doctor saw me in the state I presume I was? Are you sure he examined me? Officer, are you sure you helped me in any way, that is, by insisting that the Doctor should see me and give me treatment as an emergency case?" I asked.

"What would I have done?" she asked in return.

"What would you have done? Officer, are you sure your police station did not sentence me to death and indirectly carried out the execution by exposing me to the elements of nature to do it without blame?"

"Did we send you into crime? You blame the police instead of blaming yourself. Please mind your business".

"How else can I mind my business? My fate is in your hands. I wonder whether you are a human being. Anti-tetanus and anti-venom drugs must be available even in dispensaries to treat patients promptly. Does tetanus make a rendezvous with a patient? Officer, can snake poison wait for an unconscious patient to regain consciousness before it moves up to the heart to do its will? Officer, examine yourself in the mirror of ethics, you are a woman like me, an Ewawian like me, a human being like me. If all other things had prevented you from being kind to me, would that curse of being a woman, not have compelled you to look beyond your nose? But I am scandalized by the way the advantaged woman looks low on the disadvantaged one. Sister, the greatest enemy of a dog is a dog,"

I howled at her.

"Address yourself to the hospital staff and stop moralizing. Even if the drugs were there, they would be for good citizens and not for criminals. So address yourself to the Doctor and not to me. I am here to make sure you don't escape and not to look for medicines for you," she said scornfully.

A type of sick horror took possession of me. I eyed the officer sideways and tried to turn away from her. The stretcher on which I was laid was a coarse hard sheet of rusty iron. It was hurting my back. As I tried to turn to relieve my aching back, I nearly slipped off. A slimy greasy substance, in fact coagulated blood was all over the stretcher.

At first, I thought it was my blood. But when I ran my hand on the wound, I found out that the blood had caked - gluing the edges of the handkerchief (the policeman had used in tying the wound) firmly onto my skin. The wound might have stopped bleeding before I got to hospital. So, I thought I had wounds all over my body. There were welts all over but they did not bleed. I called the officer's attention to my plight and asked her to help turn me. She said that was not her job. She instead called the nurse. She came promptly. When she saw me, she growled, and calling the emergency ward worker said: "Evinna, are you mad? Didn't I tell you yesterday not to allow the relatives of the woman who had a stillbirth go away without washing this stretcher? Where were you when this woman was brought? See where the police dumped her. I have told you, if you don't want to work you should tell your brother who employed you here that the work is nasty for kings like you. Come on, clean the stretcher yourself".

Evinna pouted and moved away unperturbed. The nurse's revelations clicked open my sense of smell. I felt as if my nostrils were being stuffed with some solid current of fetid air emanating from the drain of a slaughterhouse. I dragged the cloth that was covering my lower section onto my face and covered it. That worsened the situation. The cloth, having been dragged on the stretcher, and being wet, carried the smell I was trying to avoid. I pushed it back and tried another method of avoiding inhaling the stench. I tried to hold back my breath as long as I could. At first I could do it for a minute, then half a minute but whenever I released the breath, I had to inhale deeply, very deeply, thus taking in four times what I was trying to avoid. So, I gave up and settled for the inconvenience.

The Doctor came in again after doing handing over rounds with his colleague. He saw the prescription in my hand and asked whether I had sent for the drugs. I told him I had no money. Furthermore, even if I had the money, I could not have bought the drugs in a state of shock. The Doctor eyed me with mixed feelings and left without saying another word. The female police officer probably angered by the nurse's remark against her people was now brooding over something. I saw her pulling faces and I thought of calling the nurse to congratulate her for admonishing the people of the First Province.

Anyway, that was not my preoccupation. I gathered courage and got up. To my shock, I got the grim reality. The cloth with which I was covered was the one I had tied my son's body in, and thrown into the lake. How did it come to be there in hospital? I remembered vividly that the frogmen had retrieved the body still firmly wrapped in it. I also remembered that before the assault on me, the body was lying a few metres away from where I was being interrogated, still very well wrapped up. A thousand things ran through my mind. I called the officer five times before she cared to answer and come.

"Please officer, where is the body of my child and why is this cloth here?" I asked.

"We brought you and the corpse here - you for treatment, and the corpse for post-mortem. Since the hospital has nothing, we took the cloth from the corpse and covered you with it, corpses don't need coverings, do they?" she responded rather light-heartedly.

My bowels convulsed. My whole system took a jolt. I trembled in anger and stammered -"And whe's, whe's, where is the body of my, my, my son?"

"Your what? Your what? Your son? Son? The body now belongs to the state and not to you," she scoffed.

"What state? A state that can't provide vaccines for children, that has hospitals without medicines, and brutal police that beat to kill innocent citizens? A state whose leaders deprive victims of disasters of relief supplies? What state? What state, officer? Does it take the death of my child for the state to show concern for him?" I asked and moved toward her. She sensed possible attack and kept quiet. That defused me and perhaps made her have second thoughts.

"The corpse is in the mortuary," she said rather sympathetically.

"Sister," I called her, being more reconciliatory. "Please sister, take me to the mortuary. Take me to the mortuary if you share in this curse called woman."

She stared at me for a couple of minutes. At that point it

seemed as if there was telepathy between us. Our two hearts now met in the curse – being a woman. Something mysterious shook her. She called out at the nurse and ordered her to take me to the mortuary. When we got there, the mortuary assistant opened the door. I dashed in alone - blind, deaf, in fact, insensitive to the horrors of the mortuary. On a platform on the left, scores of children's remains were displayed for identification. They were the remains of the Ndam fire disaster. Some of them were in a very advanced stage of decay. They emitted repulsive stench. I believe that was what held the assistant and the nurse back. On my right, I saw my son's remains apparently thrown there. I picked them up and kissed and hugged them tenderly. Tears of great remorse streamed down my cheeks as I called the dreaded name, Joseph, Joseph, Joseph. I carried my son's corpse in my hands and dashed out of the mortuary. Where was I taking the corpse to? I didn't know. I just wanted to be with Joseph even in that form. The mortuary assistant, a frail drunken fellow tried to stop me. I pushed him and he fell against the wall. He got back to his feet within a split second and attacked. He seized the legs of my son and we started tugging. The fellow I had thought was frail displayed masculine prowess. He tugged hard and pulled me to a good distance toward the mortuary. At this point he started feeling victory and pulled even harder. To prove him wrong and to settle the matter once and for all, I made a sudden hard pull with the intent of making him abandon a tug-of-war he could not win. There was a squelch, my hair stood on end as I feared we had pulled apart, the limbs of my son. I let go, and the fellow crumbled five metres away from me, bashing the remains of my son on the ground. "*Awuu!*" (He has killed it) I exclaimed in my vernacular and girded for another go at him. The policewoman, now my sister in being woman, came and pleaded with me to abandon the contest for the corpse.

"Sister, please give back the body. The post-mortem will help prove your case. So don't take the body. Let's go back to the ward," she said reassuringly.

On hearing those kind words, I surrendered to the mortuary assistant the body of my child. I saw him hold it by the legs (head down) as one holds a chicken in the market. When he got into the mortuary, he threw it onto the platform and rushed out, probably running away from the stench. We threw insults at each other and as we moved towards each other again, the policewoman came and dragged me from the place. We then returned to the ward. There was no Doctor there to attend to me. After waiting for some time, my sister in being woman took me back to the police station. Under normal conditions, or customarily, I would have paid the fare for the two of us. But because of our new-found relationship, she paid the fare and even gave me breakfast by the roadside.

When we reached the police station, I found that the ASP had done the cross-examination and was just waiting for me to sign. I moved up to his desk and signed the statement without caring to read it. That co-operation endeared me to all of them. The ASP called one of the Inspectors and asked him to take me to prison to await trial there rather than in their overcrowded cells.

2

The van that was to take me to Bondange Central Prison was parked in front of the police station. But, for two hours the officer keeping the keys of the cells was nowhere to be seen.

Some criminals who had been locked up in the cells for two weeks were also to be sent to the prison to make way for scores of fresh ones. I started developing crams in the feet. The pain in my head throbbed excruciatingly. At last, the fellow came stinking with alcohol. He staggered to the gate of the first cell and opened it. A solid mass of fetid air from the cell buffeted my face. "Horrible! Are there human beings in there?" I asked myself. To my surprise, twenty two Ewawians limped out of a two by three metre cell. All of them young men driven into crime by unemployment.

Soon, we were led into the van and transported to Bondange like fish in a cooler. There were six girls and sixteen boys in the first trip. On the way, we the girls had a nasty experience. The boys stunk like rotten meat. Some of them had developed loathsome skin diseases. Some were sloughing, others were sore in the armpits. Stripped to bare pants and having had no toilet tissue to keep themselves clean after nature's call, they stunk with faeces. Yet, they pressed on us, and thought of stupid things under those conditions. Sometimes men can be disgustingly nasty. I threatened the infidels and warded off their impudent approach on the girls. Bullshit. They knew I was stronger and healthier and I could wrench the breath out of them if they tried it.

Upon arrival at the prison yard, the boys were sent to the male-only section, and we were sent to the female-only section. A heavily barbed wire fence separated us. Thus, I started a new life, if life I should call it. I had prayed that tetanus should enter my wound and kill me without blame being laid on any person. But it did not. Nobody cared that I had a police inflicted wound. The wound was never treated. After two weeks it healed on its own, perhaps by some mystical enzyme that heals the wounds of the insane. When the scar sloughed, there were signs that the seat would puff and make me carry man-made ugliness. Although I had no reason to look beautiful, I thought I had the right to remain and be buried the way God had made me.

In the early days of my life in prison, I was twice visited by lawyers who wanted to know more about me than knowing my name Lucia, my physical appearance and my age. Because I refused to talk about my parents, my education, religion and all that nonsense, they accused me of being unco-operative, obstinate and repulsive in manners. They threatened they would close my case file. And it seems they did close, for, I remained locked up without trial for two years. I was locked up for two years, not my father nor my mother, nor my religion, nor my education, but I, Lucia - composed of my physical being which is subject to torture and my name which the media used to identify my physical being. This was what I thought mattered but the lawyers thought otherwise and so we disagreed.

At first, I used to shy away from public view because I thought the media had done a mess of me. But as time went on, I became prone to the thinking of the public. Shame did not exist any more. I tolerated the hogwash of prison life, ate the swine feed and braved the media coverage of my crime.

The first two months of my detention were without incident. The prison gates were virtually open especially to obedient inmates, those who never attempted to escape. The Senior Superintendent of Prisons (SSP) hired out the prisoners for his personal gain. Most were sent to his rubber, palm and pineapple plantations. Skilled prisoners built houses for the Ministers while the unskilled did washing and other odd jobs. Female prisoners did laundry in private homes, clinics and hotels. The lucky ones did cooking. Whatever job they did they liked it because they could take some time off for their private interests. Most of them used the time to meet their boyfriends and so satisfy the most disturbing element of human life.

Outing was the main stay of prison life. It provided the inmates with the basic life requirements. The female inmates acquired their toiletries - the curse of being a woman under such conditions. They also acquired assorted merchandise, supplementary food, tobacco, drinks (beers of all sorts, whiskies of all sorts, haah, kiikii, and drugs of all sorts) for the booming evening market in the open courtyard. They also brought stories for entertainment especially about the top strata of Ewawian society. There was no secret about a Minister or top ranking military or police personality that inmates did not know about. Although those of us awaiting trial were never allowed out, we also benefited from the outing. Firstly, we enjoyed ample space once the gates were open. Secondly, we could buy supplies from those who went out. Thirdly, we always ended up eating their swine feed, and if one had good relations with them she could have even cookies from town.

But in the third month, a very sensitive political prisoner

escaped. An order calling for maximum security issued by the Ministries of Territorial Administration, and Justice, sealed the prison gates. This turned the prison into a grim shadow of death. The SSP had relied on outing as a way of running the prison and had used up the budget on what? Only he and space knew. Now, with the gates sealed he saw a catastrophe in the making.

Rumours had it that he had fought frantically to get more funds from Government but with the ruined economy, he had failed woefully. The prisoners were now caught in a terrible quagmire.

In two weeks, hunger and malnutrition set in and reduced the once plump inmates to skeletons. The badly nourished skins succumbed to loathsome diseases - scabies, yaws and boils. I fell victim to a nondescript one. I was sloughing like a snake. In spite of the limited space, each inmate tried to avoid contact with others. Anger flared up frequently if either by accident or intent, an inmate touched another. We had no soap with which to bathe ourselves. There was no toiletry for personal hygiene. So, the stench from scabies and other bodily wastes floated solidly in the air making breathing very difficult.

By the third week, the toilets were completely blocked.

They had never been in good repairs anyway. But during the open-gate period, since most inmates went out, they were manageable. During the closed-gate period, they were used every second of the day. Worst still, disgruntled inmates started dumping whatever sanitary wear they used into them. Thus, handkerchiefs, old pants and headbands were dumped and forced into them with sticks. If one flushed a toilet, the old and the new contents would whirl up, creating a vortex of faeces that gurgled for some time then ended up overflowing the bowl like boiling *kuachah* (corn beer).

One night a terrible thing happened. An inmate sabotaged the pipes and flooded the toilets. Because they were built on higher ground than the rest of the compound, the whole place became a pool of faeces. Two days later, there was an outbreak of cholera. Before the authorities showed any sign of concern, hundreds of lives had been lost. I owed my survival to Setania, a queenly lady who had been brought in on the eve of the sealing of the gates.

Setania, it was alleged, had been awaiting trial for ten years. She was charged with killing her husband and throwing the body into the Pwalanga River about a hundred kilometres from Dande. There was a rumour that she was virtually bedridden and therefore always in hospital. But as it turned out, the SSP with the complicity of the Minister of Finance and the Director General of the Central

Bank, gave her the leeway to remain in hospital in the day and at night meet the dignitaries of Dande with whom she transacted complex businesses. For fear of his tricks being discovered, the SSP ordered her to return to prison when the sensitive political prisoner escaped from prison.

Upon her arrival, she made me her attendant. I did her laundry and so had the opportunity to use her soap in keeping myself clean also. Furthermore she had a good supply of mineral water and descent food. With such facilities, my health improved greatly and she plunged me into trade. At night, she would be taken away and brought back very early at dawn. She would bring so much supplies that several inmates would be called to carry them to her special cell. Then she would assign me to sell them at exorbitant prices. She was now the only link between the inmates and the outside world. Her trade yielded cash, real cash. I never lost one franc and so she gave me all her confidence.

It seemed to me that at that time she was aiming very high as she bribed her way into the sphere of influence. She gave lots of gifts to the SSP's family. She could order him to carry out certain reforms. She forced him, so to speak, to repair the toilets. Things started changing for the better. I, her attendant, also had some influence. But like all such situations some jealousy started smouldering among the inmates. She increased her business a hundred folds. With improved conditions, marijuana and other drugs were in high demand. She brought them in, in large quantities.

One night she said I should accompany her out. Although I longed for outing, I thought the risks were many at night. I would have very much welcomed such an invitation in the afternoon especially during the open-gate period. So, I told her of my limitations and why I could not go out that night. She insisted. After a long debate, I accepted.

We soon left for the unknown in a Mercedes car which acted as a visa. It simply glided through police checks. When we got to town, we moved from one Minister's house to another, from one Director's house to another, from one Commissioner's house to another, from one General's house to another and from one Banker's house to another. In each house we were sumptuously entertained with food and assorted drinks. At last, we went to what she called, "dealers" - lepers and the handicapped sleeping in makeshift shacks along the streets of Dande. It was about 2.30 a.m., time I thought the disadvantaged would be fast asleep. But no, it was the time they carried out big business. Whenever we got to a shack and the occupant was asleep, Setania would screech, and the fellow would get up in routine style and give her a bundle. In most cases the vendors were on hand. Within a split second Setania had purchased or taken on credit what we could ferry through the gates of the prison.

The boy the Minister of Finance gave us to help arrange the merchandise in the car was a jolly good and strong fellow. When he finished arranging the things, we left for the Minister's house to bid him good-bye. Setania was in very high spirits. She had got most of the rare drugs inmates demanded. But she had a major problem - how to carry them across, how to get them into the prison yard. As I had pointed out, some inmates were jealous of her influence and had written petitions against her. So, counter forces were constantly sent to monitor her movements. Would they be there by the time we returned? She did not know. So, she called me and told me what we had to do. Her customary practice under such conditions. We had to stuff our most private parts with the rare drugs and after crossing the check points, rush to the toilets to deliver, what she herself called, "giving birth to money".

That was the most horrible and degrading experience I have ever had in my life. The Bible says that the woman was the last created thing. So, she was the sum total of creation. If God found creation good, He found it good in the woman. She was not made from dust but from flesh. And by virtue of having been made from flesh she's more refined than the original flesh. To keep creation good she was given the powers to procreate through an awesome apple - an apple which both angel and man had, have, and will always succumb to. Now, Setania and myself were to degrade the essence of womankind for money. We stuffed our apples with capsules of marijuana, cocaine, and other drugs and were driven back to the prison yard. Our ordeal was useless. The Special Forces were not around. Our guards, that is, the usual warders who all benefited from Setania's trade, allowed us in without checking us. Once we got in we rushed to the toilets and laid the capsules.

I got so disgusted with the experience that I told Setania that I wouldn't try it again. I did not mind whether that would sever our relationship or not. I told her that there should be a degree of woman dignity that money shouldn't buy at all. That dignity had to be preserved under all circumstances. She turned crusty and accused me of moralizing the trade.

"If you find anything wrong with what we have done, then it is because the evil is deep seated in your heart. There is nothing wrong with making money. There is no code of conduct in making money. If you can make money with the Bible, do so. If the Bible impedes you, leave it and make money. Money, money," She lectured.

"That is rubbish," I scoffed and eyed her scornfully. "I can't go on a self degrading spree. I better die of hunger than do what spites womankind. Yes, I can't degrade myself for forty pieces of silver."

Setania tended to whirl with anger. She tended to regret for having taken me out. She inhaled deeply and while exhaling said rather sententiously, "Your deliverance may well depend on what you abhor." She eyed me sideways, moved away, and shut the gates of our relationship. For several weeks, neither of us spoke to the other. Yet, whenever we met, something, a mysterious feeling tended to tell each of us to ask for reconciliation. One afternoon, Setania capitulated. She greeted me and asked me to see her. I responded positively and we reconciled on my terms. I was never to be coaxed into any trade that would dishonour my kind and me.

One week after that, she took me out. We bought assorted things and after visiting several dignitaries left for the prison. On our arrival, one of the guards intercepted our car and took us behind the prison wall. He said we should wait there till he came for us. Setania at once suspected that the Special Forces were around. We hid behind a small bush for about two hours at the mercy of mosquitoes. When the guard came, we thought our ordeal was over. It was not. It had just started. The guard told us that he had to dig a hole through the prison wall for us to enter the yard. The Special Forces were combing the prison in search of Setania and were getting convinced that she had as usual slipped out of prison. When finally the hole was dug, we got into the yard and Setania pretended she was suffering from diarrhoea. The guards jubilated as Setania emerged from a toilet.

They ran to the Special Forces and announced that the lady they were looking for had not in fact slipped out of prison but was in the toilet.

These happenings distracted us to the point that Setania forgot she had to go and lay the capsules. I also forgot to remind her. At about midday, she told me she was dizzy and wanted to lie down and sleep. It is bad to be naive in certain situations. I simply approved of it and she went and lay down. A few minutes later, I heard her snoring abnormally. I went to get her up. To my surprise, she was foaming in the mouth and breathing heavily. I yelled and dashed to tell the guard who had dug the hole into the wall of the prison. He came promptly, saw the desperate situation and went and told the SSP. When the SSP saw the situation, he phoned the Director of the Central Bank and the Minister of Finance. Within a split second, an ambulance arrived and Setania was rushed to hospital. About an hour later, news came that she had died on the way to the Reference Hospital.

Setania's sudden death sent tempestuous shock waves through the prison. The SSP was shaken, really shaken. He walked with a stoop. The whole prison yard was rocked in waves of rumours, each rumour monger claiming authenticity about the cause of death. Presently, I found myself being isolated. Whenever I went to a small group discussing the death, they flicked glances at each other, ended the conversation and dispersed. After three futile attempts to commune with them, I gave it up and decided to mourn the loss of a friend alone. Once I was seized by emotions of lunatic proportions. I burst out crying aloud. A nasty lady came along and told me not to wreck the peace of the institution. Another joined her to rebuke me.

"Stop pretending to cry. Who does not know that it is your mother who is dead? If you did not want her to die, why did you poison her?" she asked jeeringly.

"Heh! Some people are shameless. If you kill somebody today, tomorrow you will follow him. There is no other way. You will also die. What a shame!" the other exclaimed.

"Poor Setania! A crab is killed with its pincers. A baboon that strikes its chest, invites the hunter. Can you imagine her assassin?"

The inmates clucked in unison, and left. Before I had time to reflect on what they had said, and link it with me, the SSP sent for me.

"Your friend died while being evacuated to the hospital. Her body is in the mortuary of the Reference Hospital. How do you feel?" he asked.

"Terribly aggrieved," I responded.

"What actually happened?" he asked.

"When we returned from outing, she told me she was dizzy and wanted to sleep. She went to bed and started snoring abnormally. So I went to shake her and get her up. But when I got to where she was sleeping, I saw her in a very bad state. So, I called the warder who came for you," I explained.

"You will help a team of investigators. Please, do your best to co-operate," he sort of advised.

My bowels turned at the word, "co-operate". I remembered my

ordeal at the police station, saw the link between the inmates' remarks and the SSP's, and once more felt the spikes of torture at the gates of my life. My countenance did not change however. I bore nobody any grudge. Everybody was right to suspect that I killed Setania. After all, when we fell out, the rumour was that we were fighting over the Director of the Central Bank.

The team of investigators came the next morning. After the formalities of giving one's name, place and date of birth, parents' names and occupation and all that rubbish, (which I of course refused to honour in its entirety) they started to question me. They asked me where, when, and how I knew Setania. They asked about our lives, the clash of interest and our reconciliation. They asked how I felt about her death, what I knew about it and why I could not alert the authorities on time to save her life. I told them the role Setania had played in saving my life during the prison catastrophe, how I became her attendant and trade assistant first, within the confines of the prison yard, and later on, outside the yard at night.

"Who allowed you out at night?" they asked.

"Setania had the licence. I don't know how she did it. She could take any woman out at any time in the night," I responded.

"What caused the breach between you?" they asked.

"The ethics of the trade. The violation of my selfhood," I responded.

"What do you mean by that? What do you say is your level of education?" they asked.

"In the night trade one loses her self-respect. Life loses its meaning," I responded.

"Why are you in prison?" one of them asked apparently out of point.

"I am not yet sentenced. I am remanded in custody," I responded.

"For almost three years!" the other exclaimed perhaps surprised by the information he had had from records, since I had refused to talk about my place of birth, parents, occupation, religion and all that nonsense.

"Why were you remanded in custody?" they asked almost in unison.

"The records have the facts," I responded.

"You had killed before, you might have killed again," one of them sneered in anger.

"You are pretty insolent. We need your co-operation.

Remember, this is not a joke," the elderly officer said.

I felt the bite of insult overwhelm my reasoning. The prison office where I was being interrogated whirled with me. I, Lucia, shut up and refused answering any other questions. The investigators gave me a stabbing look, closed their files and left. Then a wardress came and took me to a one square metre cubicle and locked me up. The faeces (of former occupants) which had caked on the floor emitted a terrible odour. The cell was dark, the walls were coarse and the ventilation so poor that I could hardly breath. I don't know for how long I remained in the cell. The days and the nights were the same. One second was one hour, one hour was one day, and one day was one week. In fact, I lost track of memory. I, Lucia, my form and my name, was put in a cell perhaps awaiting another trial.

3

I identified the days with the noise inmates made, and the nights with the chirping of insects and the hooting of owls. So I slept when I thought it was night and woke up when I thought it was day. But in most cases, I slept. This does not mean that I had a bed of roses. No, far from that. The cubicle was built for the occupant to stand and not to sit or lie on the floor. It was an invention to counter accusations of prison brutality. It was meant to kill the body and the soul without inflicting welts which Human Rights Organizations could use as evidence to protest against the maltreatment of inmates. The cubicle was one square metre large, with a two metre high metal gate. The gate was perforated at about 10cm from the bottom and 10cm from the top, perhaps to let air in and out. Midway, at about the reach of my shoulders was an opening big enough to accommodate a saucer. It could only be opened from outside. Inward there extended a shelf-like projection meant for holding objects like pans, cups and bottles. Once the wardress opened it and put the object of interest on it, she shut it again in a mad hurry.

Immediately I got into the cubicle, I realized my debacle. In such situations, anger and self-pride must be converted into ingenuity. I knew that though I could not stretch myself on the floor, I could alternate standing with sitting and thereby easing up the stress of standing indefinitely. I thought I could sleep better sitting than standing. The floor was littered with dry flakes apparently of diarrhoeal origin. They emitted a pungent odour. I crushed them into powder with my feet and pressed the powder against the perforated area of the door with my left hand. It fell out and that made the air breathable. I then trained myself on how to sit down in the cubicle. I sat with knees raised at 90 degrees, my toes touching the wall in front, and my back pressing against the wall behind. In that insidious situation, my toes hurt. So, I raised them and instead pressed my soles on the wall. That eased up things. In spite of that training I discovered that sleep chose its positions to ease up strained and hurting parts of the body.

In order not to become a victim of the wastes of my body, I refused to eat and drink. I sometimes sipped water to keep what remained of me working. After hearing the wardress put and withdraw objects on the projection four times, which I presume corresponded to four days, I heard her remark, "You don't eat. Do you think if you die there the world will end?" I did not respond. Even if I wanted to, she was not there. She spoke as she was moving away with perhaps the saucer containing the previous day's food. I might have dozed off soon after, for it was not long when a current of offensive fresh air rushed into the cubicle woke me up and terminated the beautiful dream (of being released from prison) I was dreaming. My eyes hurt as they got in contact with light.

"Follow me," the wardress said.

"I can't get up. Please help me get up," I pleaded with her.

"Get up," she scolded and drew her truncheon. That made my hair stand on end as my body creaked from numbed joints. I managed to get up and limp behind her. She led me to a waiting van and I was whisked off to the court premises.

"Sit down girlie," an elderly State Counsel said, pointing to a chair.

I sat down while he studied his files. When he finally got what he was looking for he invited me to sit on the chair directly opposite his, across the table. He breathed in deeply and then asked me whether I could read and write. He was so friendly and fatherly that I responded that I could read and write. He then told me why I was called up, and asked whether I wanted him to take down my statements or write them down myself.

I chose the latter option.

"OK. Don't be afraid. Fill out this form then write what you know about the death of Setania.

"Please Sir, my name is Lucia, I have no parents, no Province of origin, no religion etc. I am simply, Lucia. If you won't mind, I shall write only that on the form," I said pleading.

"I have told you not to be afraid. So, fill out the form as you want. But are you sure there is only one Lucia in the world? We ask for full identification because we don't want to make mistakes. But if you say your name Lucia is sufficient, fine. Go ahead." he said.

I got the papers, wrote my name on the form, and narrated my story. I wrote how I met Setania, what we were to each other, how she saved me from the loathsome skin disease, how I became her trade assistant, how one night she took me out and asked me to stuff my private parts with drugs in order to cross the gates of prison, how that destroyed our relationship for some time, how we reconciled, and finally, the outing of the night before she died and most particularly, the delay in her taking out the capsules from her private parts. When I finished, I handed over the statement to him. He read it and asked me of my level of education. I kept quiet.

"Do you think Setania might have died of drug overdose?" he asked.

"I don't know. I am not a doctor," I answered.

"Don't you think the delay in taking out the drugs might have made the capsules dissolve in her and so over-drugged her?" he asked again.

"I don't know. It had been her trade for a long time. I don't know," I responded rather confused.

"Why are you in custody?" he asked.

"The facts are in my file," I answered.

"Is your file here already?" he asked.

"I think so. I have been detained for years without trial," I said.

"About two years? Nobody is following up your case?

How do you find your stay in prison? You should have had even a boyfriend to follow up your case. You can't keep staying in prison. What really happened? You see, there are too many cases before us and only those that are pursued are tried fast. Do you say you don't have even a friend? That is horrible," he remarked.

"I have no person. I should not have been bothered to wait. But the fact that I am locked up in a cell in the prison since Setania's death, worries me considerably. I am in prison within a prison." I said.

"You are locked up in a cell?" Why do they lock you up?" he asked.

"Because they suspect that I killed Setania,"

"OK, we have the facts. Go, they will not put you in the cell anymore," he said.

After that cross-examination, I was led to the van again and driven to prison. On arrival, the wardress told me to join the inmates who were cleaning the drainage in front of the prison yard. Although I was pretty weak from hunger, I preferred working than going back to the cell. So I moved to the group and sat down on a stone. It seemed the other inmates did not take note of my presence. They started discussing me.

"I pity that girl. She is dying for nothing. The culprits of Setania's death are moving about freely while an innocent girl is suffering. Poor girl." The most elderly said.

"That is how the world is. The Minister of Finance and the Director General of the Central Bank have killed Setania and now the whole world is blaming that poor girl. This country is brooding on an active volcano," the second elderly interjected.

"My sister, see, last week when I was doing laundry for the wife of the Minister of Justice, the wife of the Minister of Territorial

Administration came in to gossip with her. They said that the Minister of Finance and the Director General of the Central Bank had wanted to introduce false currency into the economy of the country. This was to be done by way of the Central Bank acquiring billions of false Ewawian currency from Hong Kong and putting the money in circulation in the different commercial banks in Ewawa. Since Madam Setania's husband was the Assistant Director General of the Central Bank any such transaction had to pass through him. When the Minister and the Director General suggested that to him, he refused to participate in their diabolic bid to dupe the country", a light in complexion woman said.

"What!" the elderly woman exclaimed.

"I am telling you the truth. The Assistant Director General advised that because the country was recovering from a terrible economic crisis, the introduction of false currency would undermine international confidence and send away foreign investors who were beginning to trickle into the country. The Minister and the Director General then started looking for ways of eliminating the Assistant Director General", the light in complexion woman went on.

"Terrible, terrible! Do you see how fowl those big people are? People who have money!" the elderly woman exclaimed and sat down on a stone.

"Our big people are really blood mongers. After several futile attempts on the life of the ADG, the Minister of Finance promised making Madam Setania the ADG of the Central Bank if she eliminated her husband. Elated by this, she hired tugs to assassinate her husband and dump his body into the Pwanaga River. Unfortunately for them they ran out of luck. The police caught them just when they threw the body into the river", the light in complexion woman added.

"Thank God they caught them. They can't escape the death sentence", the elderly woman said jubilantly.

"You know what? The thugs were sentenced to death and executed but Madam Setania was remanded in custody indefinitely", the girl cut in.

"What! Do you see how God works in a miraculous way? Where is Setania now? Has she not died like a chicken?" the elderly woman asked rejoicing again.

"Before Setania died, there was an undeclared war between the Minister of Finance and the Minister of Justice. Whenever the Minister of Justice insisted that Madam Setania be tried, the documents got missing. The Minister of Justice in collaboration with the Minister of Territorial Administration sent several Special Forces to prison to foil Madam's outings, but they always failed. It may be the Minister of Justice was gradually catching up with them and they decided to eliminate her to cover up. As the saying goes, 'When the upper and lower teeth chew discordantly, they chew the tongue'. And that is it. Poor Setania!" the light in complexion woman exclaimed.

Although I knew that the inmates were well informed about a million events, especially those concerning the dignitaries of our society, the way the State Counsel questioned me made me draw inferences. I concluded that because Setania had not taken out the capsules from her private parts on time, they had dissolved in her and killed her. The court knew about it perhaps from post-mortem results. And that was perhaps why the State Counsel took my interview so light-heartedly. Although I had heard of the false money story and thought it was true, I did not believe the story that the Minister of Finance and the DG of the Central Bank had killed Satenia.

Two things that have been bothering me ever since are; can human imbecility ever end with regard to the greed for money? How can the Minister of Finance and the Director General of the Central Bank of a country, people entrusted with the most revered confidence of the country to handle its financial life-wire connive to ruin a recovering economy? How can people swimming in money want more through trickery? Can any of them sleep on two beds at the same time? Can anyone of them eat the food of four people at the same time? What was really wrong? Secondly, if the leaders of a country could be so heartless in dealing with each other, can any stroke of magic change their attitude towards us the lowly? No doubt our police force is trained to brutalize us the way it does, our hospitals are death traps and our prisons are simply meant to execute what the police and the hospitals leave undone.

I still have a degree of respect for Setania; I still owe her my life. In the mirror of time, I see her as a great lady. But any woman who undermines her selfhood for money, is not worthy of being God's last created being - a being that is the hub of creation, a being to which angel and man succumb alike, a being of awful excellence and reverence, and therefore a being that must respect itself and its kind more than any other.

I pity Setania for what she was. She loved money and died by and for it. In her dying she leaves nobody with the guilt of letting her blood, she died in her own way and that, I very much appreciate.

4

Two weeks after my encounter with the state counsel, I was called up to the court. Setania's matter had blurred mine in my mind. So I thought I was going to be given a formal charge for killing her. To my surprise however, I was charged of infanticide and dumping of the remains of my son into the municipal lake.

"Lucia, on 20th March, 1999 at 2.30 a.m. you were arrested for throwing the remains of a child you had killed in the municipal lake, are you guilty or not?" the judge asked.

"Your worship, there are two charges in what you are saying. I plead guilty of one and the other, I plead not guilty," I responded.

"Which of the two do you plead guilty? By the way who is your lawyer? Who is standing for you?" he asked.

"I have no lawyer, Your worship," I responded.

"This is not a simple case. This is a criminal case with the possibility of a death sentence. So, this honourable court cannot hear your case without a defence lawyer. Do you want me to adjourn the case to give you time to look for a lawyer?" the judge asked.

"No, Your worship. I have been almost three years in custody. Even if I am given another five years I shall be unable to hire a lawyer, for one thing, I have no money, I have no parents, nor capable friends. For another thing, if I get a lawyer he will concoct facts and tell lies to free me from court decision. But if I defend myself, I shall tell the truth and allow the court to take its decision," I said rather firmly.

"So, you mean you are ready to shoulder the consequences of your self-defence. Which of the two counts do you say you are guilty of?" he asked.

"I am guilty of throwing the body of my son into the municipal lake. I did not kill my son. He died on his own," I responded.

"Can you tell this court then what happened?" he said.

"On 19th March, 1999 I returned late with my sick child from Etambeng, a village about 60km from here. When I got here, I went with the child to my father's compound but I could not get in because they refused to allow me in. So I left for my foster mother's compound where I thought of spending the night and taking my son to the hospital the next morning. His temperature rose very high. I felt the heat as I carried him on my back. He was groaning as I went on. After some time, I realized that the groaning had stopped and that the child was still and cooling down as I moved on. Soon, I noticed that he had urinated and the urine had rolled down my small of the back, down down my buttocks, making me uncomfortable. Then, his legs started getting cold and dangling abnormally.

The storm in me numbed my senses. I did not think of the possibility of my son dying. I just thought he had slept, and so, wanted to go on and on till I got to where I was going. But after some time I got frightened because he was not breathing any more. At that time I was by the municipal lake. I put down my load and unslinged my son from my back. To my consternation, I realized that he was dead. For the first time in my life, I came face to face with death. A human being, my son, was dead on my back. I was alone. I had given birth to him 'alone', I had carried him from the hospital alone, and now, I was to carry his corpse alone to the unknown. I contemplated on what to do.

Several things raced in my mind. I was split between continuing with the dead child to my foster mother's house and throwing the corpse away. Considering the circumstances that led to my going to Etambeng, I ruled out bothering my foster mother. I then thought of throwing the child in the bush but on second thought I feared dogs would eat the remains. I thought of carrying the corpse to the Ministry of Social Affairs and throwing it there but when I tried to carry it on my back again, it flexed uncontrollably and for the first time I was gripped by fear. I thought of scooping a shallow grave by the side of the lake but that too proved difficult. I had no spade. So I decided to bury my son in an unmarked grave - the municipal lake where I was to throw wild flowers every anniversary of his death.

I then tied my son in the very cloth I had used to tie him on my back. I had only a fifty francs coin with me, my only treasure. I put it in his right palm and prayed that God should give me the strength to haul him far into the lake where it was deep enough to swallow him up forever and ever. I did not want my son's body to be visible in the shallow shores of the lake where it would be discovered and exploited to make headlines for the media. I wanted the loss of my son to be my loss and nobody else's. Nobody had wanted him. Nobody was to know that he had gone. Only I, Lucia, had to know that he had died and was buried in an unmarked grave. So, I carried his body and moved into the lake. When I got far enough, I hauled the body with all my might and it thumped in the heart of the lake.

As I watched the body sink and conjectured how deep it would sink to my satisfaction, I saw several searchlights converging on me. The ASP and his men came and caught me. Then they wired the frogmen and they came and dragged out my son's body from the lake. I was then taken to the police station and later on, to the hospital. My greatest worry now, Your Worship, is that I don't know where my son is finally buried. If I knew, I would want to lay a rose flower on the grave before I meet him," I stated.

"Why had you to be taken to hospital?" the judge asked.

"Because the police beat me unconscious," I answered.

"Why do you sound so motherly now toward your son? There is every indication that you murdered the child and dumped the body into the lake. Now you appear to give the court the impression that you loved your son and would have taken care of him instead of killing him. Furthermore why did your father refuse you from entering his compound? You give this court the impression that he is a bad man. You don't seem to link yourself with any evil. Yet there is sufficient evidence against you for killing your son and dumping the body into the lake."

"Your Worship, I don't want to consider my father's role in the death of my child as a criminal act. If I do, I can be accused of judging him on sentiments. For one thing, when he refused me from entering his compound, I was no longer his daughter. He had severed his parental relationship with me. I simply wanted to play the prodigal daughter but his gates are much more closed than I thought. And even here, I bear him no grudge because if I do, I shall be guilty of sentimentalism. That is why I think my trial should be based on the truth and not on the logic of the law, what you call evidence. What is evidence? To the best of my knowledge, evidence is the concoction of facts. Facts are not the truth, especially facts from our police force," I said.

"Are you now contesting the competence of the judiciary system of this country? Do you by this declaration mean that this court is incompetent to try you? You see, you need a lawyer," the Judge said and conferred with the State Counsel.

"Your Worship, I can't contest the competence of this court. I respect the institutions of my country. My only problem is the dichotomy between facts and the truth. Facts can be gathered from bodily and mental torture. But the truth remains the truth; and this is my point," I explained.

"Which of them do you assign to this court?" the State Counsel asked.

I lost my train of memory. I delayed in giving a response. As I struggled to answer, the State Counsel bellowed;

"Your Worship, this court cannot tolerate wanton distortion of court procedure. If the accused shies away from getting a lawyer she should face the consequences of her decision. There is sufficient evidence before me to convict her under section 16, article 5, subheading 19, of the Ewawian penal code. It stipulates that, any person found guilty of infanticide shall be sentenced to death by hanging. The accused is guilty of first degree murder of her own son. Here is her written confession at the police station on the night of the incident. From her intransigence, this court should have no doubts of the stuff she is made of. She is a hardened criminal and I don't think our honoured and proven legal system can tolerate her kind."

The Judge picked up from the State Council. He got a document from the file and showed me the signature.

"Do you recognize this signature?" he asked.

I answered in the affirmative. I said it was my signature.

"Now listen to your statement to the police on the night you were caught throwing the body of your child into the lake. 'On 20th March 1999, at about 10.30 p.m. I killed my son because he was always sick and worrying me. I waited till 2.30 a.m., (when I thought there would be no people around) to carry the body to the municipal lake. When I got to the lake I threw the body into it. Unfortunately for me, a police patrol caught me as I was leaving the place. After making this statement, the police officer who took it down read it to me several times, and being satisfied that it was properly written I hereby sign it.' The judge then took the post-mortem examination report too and read it to me. 'Having thoroughly examined the remains of two year old Joseph, son of Lucia; I make the following findings: - Joseph had measles with accompanied sore throat, he had a fractured skull and spine, his lungs had no foreign fluids. It is difficult to say which of the two suspects - measles, and broken skull and spine, is the main cause of death. The fact that there is no accumulation of fluids around the fractured spine and no blood in the brain makes it difficult to say that the broken spine and skull is the main cause of death. From every indication, Joseph would have survived his measles'.

The court booed, and thus gave the Judge the fillip to go ahead. I raised my hand to counter that public consensus but the Judge now too full of justice pronounced justice almost immediately.

"This court having studied case No. A002/3/00, Lucia, V. the People, and basing its attention on the facts before it, facts that leave us with no reasonable doubts, hereby find Lucia guilty of

sacraments so as to be fully prepared to meet your creator whenever the time comes. Eh, eh, I want you to confess your sins and receive Holy Communion, so that the Lord your God can dwell in you again and you in Him. Tell your heavenly father your sins and ask for forgiveness and you will see the glow of His grace settle on you again," he said.

"Parson, will that cleanse me of public condemnation and bring back my son?" I asked.

"It will do lots of things, things we cannot, in our human form know," he responded.

"What do you want me to confess, Parson?" I asked.

"The truth about your situation. Express deep sorrow for it, and plead to your Lord to forgive you. Before you do so, I pray you to eat. Eat so that the food can give you physical strength that will in turn give you spiritual strength. I shall even like you to bathe so as to be clean in body, and thus clean in spirit. Don't return to your maker in dirt. Should I give you time to do that?" the Parson asked.

I smiled and adjusted myself on my bed. The Parson eyed me from the corners of his eyes to see whether he had made an impact.

"Suppose Parson, I say I have not sinned. Suppose I say I don't want to mention God in this damned thing. Suppose I say I don't want to recall my plight. Suppose I say I hate to mention my son."

"Lucia, there is e, e, e, so much e, e, e,"

"So much what Parson? You believe I have sinned. You might have been influenced by the media and the so-called justice in Ewawa. I hate to talk to people influenced by what they call evidence and facts from the police. If you had time, I would have told you my story. But you don't have time and so you can't get my story"ı

"I have time and I am ready to sacrifice more. I just want us to be frank in this matter."

"To be frank by telling lies to please the public? Even if I were to please the public, do you think Parson, that a woman like me condemned by the population can have redemption in God? Can God forgive what you Parson, cannot forgive? Does the Bible not say that what is tied on earth is tried in heaven?" I asked.

"It does. That is why I pray that what we shall tie here on earth in relation to your situation shall be tied in heaven. Yes, it shall be tied in heaven."

"And you think I can find redemption!"

"Yes, all can find redemption in God. Lucia, even you. can find redemption. Our Lord Jesus Christ died for the sins of all. His precious blood washes all the sins. He died on the cross to redeem all from sin and hell. He will redeem you, Lucia. He will redeem you."

"I am pleased to hear that but I am still e, e, e."

"I have time, Lucia. Lucia, I have time. I shall create time for you even if it means my coming here and staying from morning to evening," the Parson said emphatically.

"Then come tomorrow. Come early," I said.

"Thank you. I shall come. But promise me you will eat," he insisted.

I promised and he departed.

6

The next day, the Parson arrived pretty early, earlier than what I expected. I had eaten as I had promised him and felt a bit stronger to face the challenges of the day.

"Welcome Parson," I greeted while shaking his holy hand.

"Thank you Lucia, and good morning. Did you eat, Lucia?" he asked.

"I did eat, Parson. And I also bathed".

"That's good," he praised. "Now before we start, I want us to pray together. I want us to kneel down and ask our heavenly father to bless us and guide our meeting with His Holy Spirit," he added.

"I shall neither kneel down nor pray. But you can do your duty. Be very free to," I said.

"Why won't you kneel down and pray to your loving father in heaven?" the Parson asked passionately.

"I have no need for prayers," I answered.

"You do have. Everybody has need for prayers. See, Lucia, the human temple called flesh needs prayers. Our Lord Jesus Christ himself spent most of his time praying though he was free from sin. In the garden of Gethsemane, he asked his disciples to pray in order not to fall into temptation. You need prayers now more than ever before," he advised.

"You see, Parson, the church teaches that God is magnificent, magnanimous, all knowing and most of all, that nothing happens without His approval. So I can't associate what has happened to me and what is about to happen to me with Him. If I do, I shall not be doing so in accordance with the teaching of the church," I responded.

"Would you have believed in prayers if the church taught otherwise?" the Parson asked.

"Yes,"

"Why?" he asked frowning.

"Because that would have been more realistic and more streamlined with our earthly chores, but the God of the church is too pious to be associated with me. Or, to put it the other way, I am too sinful to lay the blames of my predicaments on an omniscient, omnipotent, and most loving God. I want to bear my misfortunes without grudge to man and God," I responded firmly.

The Parson breathed in with an apparent feeling of

disappointment. Perhaps what he thought would be an easy mission was becoming more elusive than ever before.

"Lucia, Lucia can you tell me why your life has been ripped from the love of God and man? Lucia, what for Christ's sake has put this horrible wedge between you and all humanity? Lucia, please, in spite of all other things, you should not disown your loving father in heaven. Our earthly life ends but our heavenly life lasts forever. So let us look for eternity and not for the ephemeral," the Parson advised.

"Parson, I agree with you but what do you want me to do?" I asked.

"I want you to confess your sins and receive Holy Communion and establish your good relation again with your loving father in heaven," the Parson responded.

"OK, I accept. Let's go on with the confession," I yielded and he led us in prayers.

Let's kneel down and pray,

> Heavenly father, creator of heaven and earth, most holy and everlasting father, to you do we lift up our eyes in prayers, father, that you open up our hearts and enable us to tell you how we have sinned against you and our fellow man. Father, you who are enthroned in the heavens you know what stuff we are made of. You know that without you, we can do nothing on our own. We pray that whatever situation we find ourselves in this vale of tears, you yourself should lead us through. May your spirit descend on us and lead us through these trying times, so that your will be done on earth as it is in Heaven. Father, we extol you our Lord and king, we bless your holy name, we laud your works from generation to generation, we beseech you father, never to abandon what you created and found good in, to the evil machinations of the devil. Come down then, oh most Holy Spirit upon your daughter Lucia. Sanctify her, welcome her once more into your abode that she may once again enjoy your peace. We ask this through the most precious and saving blood of our lord Jesus Christ. Amen.

"Amen," I responded from habit.

"Lucia, your loving father in heaven has now opened up his arms to receive you. Don't waste time. He is ready for you," the Parson said with a trembling voice.

"Please Parson, give me your blessings for I have sinned. It is three years since my last good confession. Since then, I accuse myself of the following sins; I drank alcohol and was raped in drunkenness. This of course meant that I committed fornication. I threw the corpse of my dead child into municipal lake. I was jealous of my friends of the First, Second, and Third Provinces who, blockheads as I still consider them, could easily pass the exams into job-giving institutions of Ewawa while those of us from other Provinces could not pass. For these sins and those I cannot remember, I beg for your absolution," I ended the confession.

"Lucia is that all? Is that all, Lucia?" the Parson asked

"I have said that for these sins and those I cannot remember, I beg for your absolution. Do you want me to invent a sin?" I responded.

"What about eh eh eh ....?" The Parson stammered.

"What Parson? The sin we committed together?" I asked with a frown.

"Lucia, the spirit of the Lord has not descended on you yet. Your confession is not complete I shall return to the Mission and ask the legion of Mary to offer Mass for you. Good bye Lucia. As I go, don't relent in prayers. I shall ask the St. Jude Apostolate, the St. Michael, St. Joseph, St. Veronica, and St. Thomas groups to pray for you," he said.

"Parson, do you think there is need for you to come back?" I asked.

"Sure until my job is done. I shall leave the ninety nine sheep for the lost one. Sure, I shall be here when I am convinced external prayers have worked," he responded.

"When the gallows might have given a dreamy smile. Good bye parson."

7

"**W**elcome Parson. Thank God you have come. It is exactly two weeks since you left here." I welcomed the Parson.

"How has it been? Fine?" he asked.

"Terrible Parson, terrible. Ever since you left, terrible things have happened here. I thank God that you have come. Welcome," I said heartily welcoming the holy Parson.

He was delighted to see me in such mood, to hear me express the desire to see him, and to see me, so to speak, in good health. I ate well and even drank whatever little drink a kind guard or visitor gave. International, especially American and European charity organizations provided assorted gifts in food and soft drinks though most of them ended up in the houses of the prison authorities.

"Thank you Lucia. I would have come earlier but I fell ill after straining myself on the new church project. Thank God that you are fine. I have come that we complete our project. I want to see you become a child of God again. You must be born again in our Lord Jesus Christ."

"Yes Parson. I accept though I know you will refuse. I have always been born again in Christ in my terms, and not in the terms of the visible church or those of the state. Any state or church that works on human evidence or police facts imprisons its conscience and loses the truth. And when that happens the state imprisons its best brains and the church excommunicates her best Christians. That is why I would have liked you to listen to my story without pre-judging it. I heartily welcome you today because of the daily happenings in this prison nowadays. It is horrible. It may be I was not frightened because I was writing for you what I have to say. I have not finished but if time catches up with me, ask the guard who ushers you in here. I shall leave everything with her. Publish it for posterity. I have even asked a charity organization to help you publish it. If you are too busy, please give it to the Canadian Mission," I said.

"What has been going on?" the Parson asked.

"You see that cage 97, the girl who was in it was executed the night of the evening you left here. She was called Yvonne Eponde. She had a degree in Political Science. While as a student, she fell in love with an American trained geologist. Upon his return to

Ewawa, he was employed by the Ministry of Mines and sent to the Far Eastern Province for gold prospecting. Within four months of prospecting, he came up with a list of minerals (gold, diamond, tin. Iron ore, copper, etc.) which the French had been mining from the region for years without the knowledge, or with the complicity of certain members of the Ewawian Government. This might have annoyed the French. He was then withdrawn from the F.E.P. and made an Assistant Director in the Ministry. In the Ministry, he was pro-American prospecting of our minerals. The Minister tended to like his arguments in staff meetings. One evening he was gunned down by an assassin. In the course of investigation, his girlfriend was told that the Director masterminded the killing So, she befriended him and shot him in the loins while they were making love. While the fellow was in agony, Yvonne told him this, 'You agent of the French, I want you to own the Ministry of Mines now and forever,' and she carried the naked fellow in a pickup and threw him at the Nkondo marketplace in the night. The next morning the population came to jeer at the fellow. The next morning, Yvonne was caught, tried, found guilty and sentenced to death.

That other cage, cage 74, the girl who was in it was executed two days after Yvonne. She was called Marie-Claire Ntonga. She had a degree in law. She was perhaps the most beautiful creature I have ever seen. While in the law school, she fell in love with an architect (Mr. Tibi Ekolo from the Sixth Province) working with the Ministry of Housing and Town-planning. The Directorate of Town-planning was then in a wooden building near Lake Bundi. Because of the then oncoming France-Afrique summit the roads of the city centre were to be widened on one side only, and full compensation was to be made to all those whose houses were to be destroyed in the process.

The architect established a list of all those concerned and sent it to the Director for onward transmission to the Minister. The Director called him and asked him to add the Minister's name, his own name (Director's) and the architect's name to the list. Mr. Tibi refused to do that. The Director forwarded the list but told the Minister what Mr. Tibi had failed to do. The next month, Mr. Tibi was transferred to the Extreme North. But before he left, he revealed to the media that on record, the Director had 250 phantom houses for lodging civil servants, for which government paid 150,000Frs. for 50; 280,000Frs. for 100; 500,000Frs. for 50; and 1,000,000Frs. for the rest, monthly. The Director had made 70 land certificates by converting Government land into his personal property, and had sold unspecified number of Government buildings to his family members and friends. All this information was backed up with tangible records. As soon as the media started publishing the information, the wooden buildings were set ablaze in plain daylight.

The Minister of Housing went on the air to blame BONEL (the Electricity Company) for poor electrification of the buildings. Computers, typing machines and other equipment worth hundreds if not thousands of millions of Frs. CFA were lost. Mr. Tibi went up to the north but came down for his wedding. Two days into his honeymoon, a waitress poisoned him in his hotel. Marie-Claire got wind of the conspirators and aided by sympathizers she also eliminated the Director without trace. It was when she tried to eliminate the Minister that she was caught, tried, found guilty and sentenced to death.

You see cage 54, the girl who was in it was the most brilliant girl I have met. When her Birmingham Professors heard that she was incarcerated in Ewawa, they hired lawyers for her. But the Ewawian Government termed her case an internal affair and did not allow the lawyers into the country. So, she refused to be defended by money mongering made-in-Ewawa lawyers. According to police evidence, she was caught helping a shot and badly wounded armed robber to escape police arrest. She did not deny the charge but said that when she was returning from Tuada International Airport at night, she met a badly wounded person (a human being) by the roadside a few kilo metres from Dande. He had bled so badly that he was slipping into a coma. So with the aid of some passengers from another vehicle she managed to put him in her car and drove him to the hospital. But on her way, she did not stop at the police checkpoint to answer the numerous questions they wanted her to answer.

When she got to the hospital, the medical staff refused to attend to the patient unless he was identified. Some even wanted money before attending to him. So, she left him there and went to her house to get money to bribe the medical staff to do their duty. By the time she returned to hospital, the fellow had died. In anger, she refused to give the emergency services her identification papers and picked up a quarrel with them, accusing them of incompetence, corruption, and murder. So, the emergency services phoned the police. As she drove homeward, the police trailed her and caught her in front of her house. She was charged of collaborating with armed robbers, found guilty and sentenced to death.

These are happenings in the condemned female section, what is happening in the condemned male section, I don't know. Let me not forget, I would have taken my turn last night. It seems as if the guards made a mistake. They opened my cage but before they carried me away one of them remarked that I was not the girl on the roll that day. They asked my name. I told them I was called Lucia. They looked at the records and left. That is why I thank God for your coming. I shall try to end my story today. Last night I was lucky. I may not be lucky next time," I concluded.

"Lucia, I am particularly happy that you are ready and willing to talk to me. Not to me as such, but through me to our Lord Jesus Christ who shed his precious blood to redeem us from sin. What you have told me so far, is irrelevant. I want us to go straight to the right thing. Let's go through this thing and find peace with ourselves and with our maker," the Parson advised.

"Rev. Parson, do you want me to confess again? What do you want me to confess? A loose girl of my age is likely to be guilty of one sin only. But I am not a loose girl. Even if I were, I am in prison, condemned to death - the thought of which alone causes fits to the weak-hearted. I pray you Parson, let me talk to you in my terms and not in yours. Mine are truthful, yours are pejorative," I said rather pleading.

"Lucia, you are not yet prepared to talk to your Lord your God," the Parson said, stood up and went without saying good bye.

8

The Parson's departure worried me greatly because by talking to him, I purged myself of certain impurities of our society. Secondly, I was sure he could publish my thoughts without money being the driving force. Thirdly, only he could be allowed to converse with inmates for hours without interruption. Was he fed up with what he might have termed my intransigence? Was I really intransigent because I did not tell him a lie that I had murdered my son? If confession meant telling the Parson what the media and police evidence had convinced him to believe then of course, I had no choice but to die with the truth about my story. After all, that is how things work in a society like ours. Poor Ewawa; and if I talk of Ewawa, I talk of the whole of Africa. I can't understand that even a white man in Africa reasons and does exactly as the native African. When a white Parson was brought to me, I thanked God that I would have the audience I needed. But the white Parson became blacker in his judgment than a black Parson would have been. One never knows the direction of a whirlwind. So I decided to continue writing my memoir for the Parson should in case my executioners caught up with me.

On the third day however, he came smiling. He brought me cookies and other baby-liking sweets. Perhaps he meant to pamper me. I accepted the gifts with the appreciation of a child to streamline their significance, so to speak, with their purpose. That pleased the Parson and established the mood of the day - the relationship between parent and child, teacher and pupil.

"Now Lucia, I want you to kneel down and we pray together before we say anything," he said.

We knelt down without a word. Then he led us in prayer.

At the end, we recited the 'Our Father Who Art In Heaven', and three 'Hail Marys'. Then he said each of us should talk to our heavenly father silently for a minute or two before opening our eyes. We did and in the end, he said Amen, and I responded Amen. Then he sent his holy hand through the narrow window of the cage, took my sinful hands and blessed and kissed them.

"Lucia, here we are - at the gate of redemption. Now, to you. Tell your Holy Father, what has created a rift between you and Him and say you are really sorry for it," he advised.

"Reverend, you insist I should confess my sin, feel sorry for it, receive the sacraments and so prepare myself for my eternal union with our creator. I would have readily done that if I had killed my son, if I had committed any crime. All I know is that the day my son died, God blinked. That is all. Yes," I said, breathed in deeply and ... I don't know.

"Lucia, Lucia, You mean you didn't kill your child?"

"Yes, of course."

The Parson winked abnormally and seemed to do some mental recollection of a number of newspaper reporting, apparent eyewitness accounts and court proceedings. He looked at me straight in the face, stretched himself, and rumbled the muscles of his throat then asked,

"Why are you then condemned to death for infanticide?"

"Because police evidence is the truth, and nothing but the truth in Ewawa. And because the court needs the truth in order to deal with the lowly truthfully, it turns to police evidence and deals with us untruthfully. This does not remove the fact that in some cases, situations like mine have turned out to reflect police evidence," I responded.

"Yes Lucia, you therefore see that the police have a very difficult job. There are hardened criminals who make it impossible for the police to view a case like yours in any other light but in the way the general situation presents itself. I am getting more and more confused with your situation. But before I take any step, I shall want you to withdraw your statement that, 'The day your child died, God blinked.' God can never blink. Blink against what, the wind, a pebble or what? He watches over us incessantly and does not blink," he remarked.

"Holy Parson, it may not be the day my son died. It may be the days, if not years that created conditions leading to the day my son died," I responded.

"I am therefore ready to listen to you. I am confused. To be candid, I am confused. I think I have to ask the Canadian Mission to do something for you before it is too late. Can you let me go? I want to see the Canadian Ambassador in his office. He has to help us appeal your case. Please Lucia, it is urgent. I must go," he said really concerned.

"An appeal will involve lawyers. They will base their argument on logic and try to convince the court that I am not guilty. The court may respond on the basis of the weight of the lawyers concerned. This to me is a distortion of the truth. So, if you are appealing, make sure you don't get lawyers for me. I shall defend myself," I said.

"Lucia, you once defended yourself but lost the case. So, let us give to the lawyers what belongs to them," he said.

"Lawyers in Ewawa?" I asked.

"Yes, even them," he replied.

"Give to Caesar what is his, even if that does not conform with Christian ethics," I responded.

"Lucia."

"Parson."

"Lucia."

"Parson."

"Lucia, there is something wrong. There is something wrong, more wrong than I think. Several things are crowding into my mind and I think the Canadian Mission and I have to review your case at different levels," he said with a frown.

"Because you think I am mad Parson?" I asked.

"No, not really but, but eh, eh ... " he said inconclusively.

"Yes because a girl like me should be mad," I said again.

"No, though I have to tackle the matter from two fronts," he said again.

I smiled and suggested that he could seek the intervention of a psychiatrist at the Nvongolo Institute.

"What is your level of education? I need to know in order to be able to assign you a certain portion of your case. The lawyers will also want to know for the same reason. As you see, your case is not a simple one at all. We have to fight against written evidence. And you know lawyers hate losing outstanding cases. Any lawyer that wins a case like yours insures success in his profession. That is why we must work together to insure success," he said.

"That is commercializing the fate of a poor girl," I said.

"For her benefit," he remarked.

"For that of the profession," I retorted.

"Which is more important - to save life or to make money?" he asked.

"I don't think that is what is important here. What I think is important is the position of truth in human affairs. If the court which is a symbol of justice should arrive at the 'truth' from panel-beaten logic, or what I may call tailored evidence then of course, its decisions can be nothing else but limping justice. A society that functions on limping justice can never win God's blessing, for, He is a just God," I said.

The Parson looked at me from the corners of his eyes and shook his heard. Something tended to gnaw at his bowels. He scratched his belly several times.

"Lucia, only the justice of God is perfect. The justice of man is relative. You see, a medical officer can x-ray broken bones but can he x-ray psychological problems? He can only observe them and draw conclusions. A judge can only base his judgement on observable facts. He cannot detect the lies a hardened criminal presents to him. So, there is quite a dilemma in justice. Often, things are never what they seem. But the world must go on. Mistakes may be made here and there. The important thing is to try and correct them. Nobody is perfect. We are all in the gloom," he lectured.

"Yes Parson, but suppose the court itself is in the mainstream of creating the mistakes? Suppose a court is so corrupt, so money minded and fearful of the regime? What will be the fate of the population especially that of the lowly? I see most of the problems of Ewawa are directly or indirectly related with the way Ewawa is governed on the one hand, and the way the laws of the country are interpreted by the courts on the other hand. The Supreme Court swears in a government. If the Supreme Court swears in a government on the wrong premise, or if it swears in a government because it has been corrupted, then of course, governance becomes dependent on the goodwill of law enforcement institutions of the nation. That of course means, giving a delivering goat to a lioness midwife. We can't call such a situation a situation that cannot be x-rayed, can we?" I asked.

"Lucia, in spite of the logic in what you are saying, I have a duty towards you. I must go and see the Canadian Ambassador. I shall see you tomorrow. May the peace of our Lord Jesus Christ be with you till we meet tomorrow," he wished, and hurried off.

9

"**P**arson, you are most heartily welcomed. I thought you hurried away the other day for good. I thought you were already fed up with me. Thank you for turning up," I said.

"You should thank God before man. May the peace of our Lord Jesus Christ be with you now and for always," he prayed, sent his holy hands through the narrow window, held my sinful hands and we both recited the Lord's Prayer.

"Reverend Parson, I think today, we should not dwell on the rights and wrongs of our judicial system, if system, I should call a bunch of uncouth and individualistic interpreters of the law. I want to tell you my story. So please, listen attentively so that you can shape it to give the picture of the death of my son as I saw it, and not as the police and the court have it in their records, to describe myself as I am, and not as the police and the court think Lucia is, to give a graphic picture of life in Ewawa as it is and not as the media tells the world it is. This is my humble plea," I pleaded with the Parson.

"That's OK Lucia," he responded.

"Reverend Parson, do you know why I shun giving my father's name, my age, my Province of origin, my level of education, my tribe, my religion and all that vileness? It is because they are pejorative. Suppose I said I was the daughter of a catechist don't you think the case would have had a tilt toward my father's vocation rather than toward its reality? Can you guess my age from what I look? If not, it is because the hardship imposed on me by the malpractices of this regime has made me older. How can knowing my age then help in determining the cause of my action in this case? If I said I was a Moslem or Christian, don't you think that will brew bias if it is a Christian or Moslem judge respectively? Furthermore, how will that reflect on the hardship which is the hub of what happened to me? Those are some of the reasons that make me consider those stigmas known as identification marks as nonsense.

Parson, to cut a long story short, let me start by telling you the socio-economic history of Ewawa. When I was a student in Upper Six, the economy was booming. Those who had coffee, cocoa, banana, that is, the farmer in general lived well. The petty-trader fared well. My father did not belong to either of those professions or any other moneymaking one. He was a catechist. Everyday he went to church and prayed for the prosperity of the nation. And God, so to speak, heard his prayers. The country was peaceful. The beggars' alms pans were full. There was respect for law and order. University education was not only free; the students received a monthly stipend.

While my father prayed in church, my mother fried doughnuts after Mass to pay my school fees. We lived in our way not actually enjoying but not suffering. I worked hard in school, really hard. While my 'well placed' friends skipped around making merry and taking risks, I remained with my natural seal.

One day in church, I decided to listen to the Lord's Prayer more attentively. When some old folks got to' "... give us this day our daily bread" they cupped their hands and raised them to heaven above and it seemed to me that their plea was carried by some astral force to God. Overtaken by that overwhelming evidence of the power of prayer, I knelt down and pleaded with God to help me pass my oncoming G.C.E. Advanced Level Examination. I saw that as a first step for a holy family too, to receive its daily bread from God the benevolent father. Results came, and I Lucy Ntang, had all my three papers in the arts.

I entered the University of Ewawa in 1981. The economy was booming. University students' stipend was increased. Married students received family allowances and even single students who happened to be with child received child allowance. There were frequent marriages. Childbirth was an honour and not a disgrace. In spite of all that, I still remained as sealed as ever. I had only one aim, complete university and work and so give God's given daily bread to my parents - His servants. Jobs could be picked from anywhere.

Then came that glorious day, the "bourse" day. For the first and last time in my life, and probably my parents' lives, I was given 90000frs. stipend. I took the money home and gave it to my parents. My father immediately developed palpitation. He became uneasy for some time. When he finally calmed down, he suggested we show the money to the Rev. Parson of the St. John of God's Parish, our Parish. In the evening we went and presented the money to him. He blessed it and kept it in the safe of the church. From that day my father changed my name from Lucy to Lucia. At the peak of his happiness he simply called me, Cia. On Sunday, he offered Mass for the family.

In 1982, the old man of Ewawa died suddenly of fatiguegosimiasis. Succession to his chair was apparently easy and smooth; for, he had so to speak, groomed an energetic young man to succeed him in case he died in his sleep. The young Saul Kilcam, took to the podium with confidence - he was more educated, more charismatic, and of course, a new broom. Yes, a new broom with great expectations. Within a few weeks he eclipsed the old dad in popularity. His pronouncements generated hope. The economy was skyrocketing, so to speak. The citizens of neighbouring countries sought refuge in Ewawa. There was a shortage of manpower especially skilled manpower. Graduates were in high demand. In 1984, I completed my studies.

I was split between doing postgraduate studies and coming out to head a Department and applying for a job at once. I thought I had to raise my parents' standard of living first before doing further studies. I thought if I worked and gave my mother a good capital, she would be able to fend for a family of four. My father did not need much money although he seemed to enjoy having it. One early morning while my mother was busy frying doughnuts, I was writing an application for employment to the Ministry of Education. All of a sudden, I heard swaih followed by the scent of fried flesh. There was a yell and a groan. I rushed to the kitchen and found my mother in a situation beyond words. She had stepped on a piece of wood in the fire and it had tipped frying oil on her. The Parson rushed her to a remote but very effective Mission hospital 80km away from Dande and I had to be there with her for two years.

By the time I came back to look for employment, the nation was convulsing in economic, moral and other crisis. My papa's land was moving from the slogan of 'strictness and uprightness,' to a creed of laissez faire and debasement. Our artists were moving from graceful dancing to skips, hops and jumps. Our musicians were abandoning rhythm for tattoos. Our lakes were exploding in anger and killing thousands. Our mountains were spitting venom. Ministerial buildings and banks were picking fire at will. School buildings were 'collapsing standing' to be later dynamited. Fortune seekers from neighbouring countries were fleeing from my papa's land. The children of my papa's land were fleeing from their papa's land. A mysterious gloom was settling on Ewawa. It seemed as if the gods had dammed the stream of prosperity that had once flowed and watered her gardens. There was total desolation. Marriage, especially among students became a taboo, childbirth was shunned. Stipends were stopped and school fees introduced.

The effects of these happenings on the population could not be described. University degrees became useless. The economy was in shambles. There was massive unemployment. Graduates became hawkers, thieves, highway robbers, loafers, harlots, feymen, counterfeiters, beggars, in fact, life in townships lost its value and there was massive urban exodus and migration to America and Europe, what was called 'bush-falling'. Everything, every transaction in Ewawa was carried out in the black market. One could feel the influence of sect practices everywhere in Ewawa. Ministers and the top brass of society were accused of homosexuality and human sacrifices. Some shameless ones went to court to clear their names and after tailoring a verdict with the judges against the accused, advised the accused behind the screens, to admit guilt and be fined a symbolic franc. Within a short time, Ewawa wore the crown of the most corrupt nation in the world.

Men of conscience moved all about with heads drooping. In that total desolation they converted every wall in the city into a wailing wall against which they sang this song of lamentation –

The Harvest Is Depleted

The harvest is depleted,
Beggars' alms pans empty,
There's want in the land of plenty,
There's cry where the milk did flow.

Oh! reign of terror, reign of calamities,
Our police beat us unconscious,
Our economy is in shambles,
Our lakes explode in anger,
Our Ministries pick fire at will,
And schools collapse standing.

Awls hoot in mournful tunes,
The sky is cast in dark ridges
There's red rain at the horizon,
And matrons mourn in tears.

Let's flee this boiler to safety,
This isn't our once dreamland,
Tell *Little John*, the Moses,
The Red Sea is verily red.

As if that wasn't enough, the scourge of HIV / AIDS reduced the once flamboyant population into frightened rodents. If one stayed for a week without seeing an intimate friend, she needed just to go round the wailing walls of the University buildings or those of the city centre and would see a picture, a picture of her friend -

dead, dead a week or so ago. Yes, dead a day of so ago - born 1982 dead 2003.

While the victims suffered, the ruling clans capitalized on the catastrophe and asked for foreign aid. As the aid poured in, they devised ways of swindling it. Doctors abandoned their specialties and became AIDS specialists overnight in order to have their share of the booty. Claims and counter claims for discovered cures superseded medical ethics. Gynaecologists and paediatricians the key medical personnel for the survival of a dying nation cajoled First, Second and Third ladies of the nation to open Foundations for the prevention of the transmission of HIV/AIDS from mother to child. The opening of such Foundations where they succeeded in building one became showcases of gorgeous dressing, wearing of the manes of lions, deification of the founders, glorification of the whole system, organization of champagne parties and declarations of motions of support for the Head of State. Then, came in the raison d'être of the founding of the Foundations - the struggle for administrative posts and contracts to build the Foundations. And once a gynaecologist, or paediatrician, usually a relative of the founder got the administrative post, or a multimillion francs contract to build the edifices, he put an end to his medical practice and became a saver of money and not a saviour of lives. Yes, he became an Ewawian, an Ewawian of the **New Contract,** an Ewawian of reversed values.

And after laying a few blocks and receiving more than 95% of the contract money through the complicity of the Divisional Officer, he abandoned the project and formed a political party - an appendage of the ruling party. And so long as he sang the same dirge with the ruling party, all was right. The project could go hang. People of conscience could go hang. Yes, all could go hang. Today, Dande is strewn with moss-covered walls of buildings abandoned by ex-medical Doctors and their likes who became contractors simply to swindle contract money. And when they did that, they sought refuge under the umbrella of the 'Presidential majority' in Parliament. In some cases, medical Doctors abandoned medical practice to become Mayors of Rural Councils in order to swindle council money and use council vehicles to build mansions for themselves. All this under the cover of the ruling party - the party of hope.

I still maintained my nature's seal. Having been used to hardship by upbringing, the crisis did not (at first) affect me as it affected my merry-go-round fellows. "There was a way out," I said to myself with armoured will. People still got employed through passing entrance examinations into institutions which led to automatic employment upon completion of their courses. So, I set myself on my books. All the money we had, had been spent on my mother's health. Though she had miraculously recovered from her third degree bums, she was virtually a living corpse. She was stiff in the joints and so walked like a wooden woman.

To prepare for one of those examinations required at least 80,000frs - a mountain of money to the poor like me. And here I was, with nature's seal, the pride of a holy family. And of course, I had to sit all the four exams to oblige God to once more send our daily bread through my hard work. This is the ordeal I faced to register for each of the examinations - Ewawa School of Administration and Magistracy, (ESAM); Ewawa Higher Police College, (EHPC); Ewawa School of Diplomacy and International Relations, (ESDIR) and Ewawa Higher Teachers Training School), (EHTTS).

-Registration fee .... 10,000frs.
-Medical certificate .... 30,000frs.
-Birth certificate .... 1,000frs.
-Certificate of nationality .... .1,000frs.
-Attestation of names 1,000frs
-Attestation of originals of *AIC* ...... 10,000frs.
-Attestation of residence 5,000frs
-Bribe in all the stages .... 15,000frs.
-Transport .... 5,000frs.
-None conviction certificate .... 2,000frs.

I sat each of these exams three times, passing the written but losing the orals. In each case of the orals, I was expected to give a bribe of 1,000,000frs. I hadn't, nor can I tell you here Parson, how I got those huge sums of money and still maintained nature's seal - the pride of my family. Only my tattooed body and the wrinkles of old age on my forehead can tell. What remained of me, the police ravaged with truncheons.

I swear to God, I swear by my mother's pains in hospital, these damned policemen who are keeping me here for the supposed murder of my child make me develop nausea whenever I see them parade the streets of this city pretending to be peace keepers. To get one document from the police station took me weeks, in spite of bribing them. I wonder what I would do if I were in a place of influence and saw in a document; Father's profession: - **Police, Magistrate, Minister,** or any of those shams - all that nonsense. Parson I am heated up. Let me take a few minutes and cool down.

Thank you for listening so attentively.

"Yes, Lucia, you are indeed, bitter," he said.

"I should be bitter. Those fellows should be in prison, not me. See Parson, while the devastating economic crises crushed the ordinary man, the leaders of Ewawa, especially the Ministers, tore down their private storey buildings worth 75,000,000frs and replaced them with skyscrapers worth billions of francs - looted state money!" I shouted and asked the Parson to give me time to recover.

10

After a break of about ten minutes, I asked the Parson whether he was still willing to listen to me. I told him that although I was capable of writing down what remained to be said, it was easier to speak than to write under the conditions and equipment I had in the cage. I begged him to bear with me and he accepted.

"Lucia, I am ready to listen to you to the end if that will make you confess and then establish that link I want you to establish with your maker. Please, avoid breaking down," he advised.

"Thank you Parson. God has blessed us today. He may not do so tomorrow if the hounds come and take me away. To continue my story; after getting frustrated with those exams, and here again Parson, I should say, it is heartrending to see bright students fail exams while leather headed ones, class-repeaters, pass with the aid of their parents' loots, positions or tribal origins. After getting frustrated with those exams, I decided to do the postgraduate course and thus come out with a qualification that would compel the government to give me a job. Although there were thousands of graduates in the streets, there were few postgraduates.

I assembled the Mvondokabi introduced school fee of 50,000frs. and registered. When I got to class, our once resplendent professors were listless. They looked like scarecrows. They rode in scrap metal in the name of cars from Europe. It seemed as if with the economic crisis, the professors were assigned to keep Europe clean by buying the scrap from there. The loose exhaust pipes, the dangling mudguards and ill fitted bonnets, boots and doors of the cars made rasping deafening noise as the cars lumbered from one pothole to another, gasping climbing the University hill. As long as one was climbing the hill, nearby classes had to stop until distance cleared the noise. In spite of that, Mvondokabi himself rode a Mercedes 800.

To further plunder the University and build for himself a five hundred million francs castle, he embarked on building a three billion francs Chinese wall round the place. He set his company to build the fence with the aim of hemming in protesting students, capturing them, and torturing them in the 5th District Police Station where he had arranged with the Commissioner to deal mercilessly with insurgents. He did not only target students. He targeted even the academic and clerical staff who dared protest against the nonpayment and drastic cuts in salaries. He summarily dismissed the clerical staff delegation that dared ask for their nine months unpaid salaries. He suspended the salaries of the professors that 'militated' in the Professors' Union - a Union he had banned. He called in troops to brutally suppress student riots. To him, every act of protest or complaint was instigated by the opposition, and was as such, aimed at toppling their government, a government which gave them the leeway to corruption and embezzlement of public funds. Insurgency had therefore, to be crushed with all the French colonial machinery of oppression they could still piece together. Dialogue would tantamount to weakness.

The students and the dismissed clerical staff reacted in like measures - violence for violence. They carried out daring acts of sabotage against the institution at night. They burnt down wooden buildings and vandalized electrical installations by stealing the bulbs and cables. They stole all moveable chairs and tables from classrooms, broke the glass windows of unprotected buildings, and destroyed the few toilets in place. They dug out the bowls and sold them in roadside markets. The campus thus became an open sewage. Every hidden corner became a toilet. The walls of buildings became urinaries. Fortunately, the campus was overgrown. If one saw a student especially a girl jump behind an overgrown bush, one had to skip away or look the other way to give her time to ease herself. As things got to a head, Mvondokabi classified urination as an act of sabotage and started looking for scapegoats. He called some of his lecturers and asked them to go round taking down the names of students and workers who defecated and urinated in the campus. The lecturers refused to carry out such mean assignment and boldly asked him whether he had any working toilets in the campus. That was of course, a direct challenge to his ego. He reeled in anger and suspended their salaries. But then, he still faced the reality. In his irrationality and total disregard for advice, he built toilets in inaccessible valleys 250 meters away from classrooms close to shacks built by native squatters at the border with the University. The muddy and overgrown paths leading to the toilets made it impossible for students to use them. So, they abandoned the toilets and started contesting on who would be bold enough to urinate in front of a full lecture hall. Before long, some native squatters moved into the toilets with their families and occupied them. When Monsieur Messling, a son of the soil replaced Mvondokabi as Rector two years later, he found it impossible to dislodge his people from the toilets. As such, while it was on record that hundreds of millions had been spent to build toilets at the University, there were no toilets.

The main library was also vandalized. Its priceless books were looted and sold by the roadside and in Muloko market. In sympathy and solidarity with their dismissed colleagues, the spared clerical staff jumbled up documents in the Admissions Offices and made it impossible for the administration to function. It was impossible to trace any document.

Mvondokabi was completely outflanked, completely beaten. All his efforts to destroy the popular insurgency failed. Everybody thought he was finished. But then, his mentor at the Presidency, the Secretary General with whom he had shared the booty of the fence-building project, stepped in and portrayed him to the President who had just returned from a three month private visit to France, as a patriot of unequalled valiancy. And so, to the surprise of everybody, Mvondokabi was promoted. He was promoted to Minister of State in charge of Higher Education. I lack words to describe what happened at the University. It was horrible. It was horrible that an American trained scholar could lead to the ruin of an institution of higher learning he had the privilege to head in that way. It is a shame how some people can be mean when possessed by the devil of greed and power. It may not even be a shame. It is standard practice that if one wants to be promoted or retained in high post in Ewawa, he must be morally bankrupt; that is, steal, or gravely offend the population.

Can you imagine Parson, that a Rector who dismantled a University garage of 150 road-worthy vehicles which he sold at 30,000fr apiece to his relatives (a garage with a 210 work force, a garage that ordered spare parts in hundreds of millions of francs, a garage that facilitated field research) could be worthy of promotion anywhere else in the world but in Ewawa?

Mvondokabi's promotion was of course, an indirect way of giving the *coup de grace* to Higher Education in the country. And in earnest that is what happened. And who cared? After all, the children of the big guns were all abroad undergoing high quality education in the US and Europe. That was necessary because it was the surest way of maintaining the status quo. So long as they received superior education, they would, upon return to the country, cow us with the aura of high quality education, and so, rule us as their parents had ruled our parents.

As things worsened, some professors got insane. Today, it is disgusting to see them forage for food in dustbins around the University restaurant. The best migrated to the United States and

Europe. At the peak of the migration Mvondokabi banned foreign travel to all University professors. The police scouted the airports and pulled out of planes even professors who could prove beyond all reasonable doubts that they were going out to attend their children's weddings in the USA or Europe. But even here, Mvondokabi failed. Determined 'bush-fallers' devised several routes to frustrate him. Some went to neighbouring countries by mami-waggons and flew from there to their destinations. Others enrolled in banned political parties and applied for political asylum in lands of freedom - especially America.

The professors who considered such manoeuvres as a waste of time and decided to brave the spiting and humiliation and stayed on, devised diverse ways of combating the tyranny and kleptomania. Some in the Faculty of Medicine strayed into traditional medicine to gamble and pinch on the meagre subsistence of traditional practitioners. The wives of most professors sold assorted vegetables and tomatoes in front of their houses to make ends meet. At dawn, their husbands sneaked to abattoir to buy dog-meat for their battered families. Worse still, some died in motor accidents on the way to buy cheap foodstuffs in bush markets.

When the Ministers of the First, Second and Third Provinces saw their kith and kin shrivel in poverty at the University, they placed them on secondment in their Ministries on fabulous allowances. The professors' conditions improved automatically and as they built up provocative multiple chins, heavy jaws, quadrupled buttocks, over-creamed bodies, and rode service Pajeros, their less fortunate and disgruntled colleagues of other Provinces came to class with sore-minds and read badly prepared notes, then left ten minutes later. With that, I knew I was wasting my time. Everything around was fake. There was misery in the faces of the lecturers. Their salaries had been slashed three times and there were no hopes for their restoration. A University with disgruntled professors is as miserable as a leprosy settlement. So I decided to lose my 50,000 Frs. and quit.

There seemed to be a vacuum in leadership. Every aspect of Ewawian life looked questionable. Governing Ewawa became akin to eating spaghetti; wrap or scoop, neither the fork nor the spoon could bring things to the point of cohesion. The so-called top brass of Ewawian society did things with impunity. Ministers, Secretary Generals, Directors of Parastatals, Rectors of Universities, Director Generals of Commercial Institutions especially the banks, Governors, Divisional Officers, Treasurers and Contractors who denuded budgets or swindled funds entrusted in their hands, and siphoned the money to Europe and America, set their infrastructures on fire and blamed poor electrical installation. Individuals became richer than the state.

Yet, at the peak of that moral decadence, that insensitivity to the suffering of the masses, the looters precipitated Presidential elections. They were under the spell of Krudi, a daring and fiery opposition leader who had cropped up from nowhere to challenge the status quo. Krudi's inroads and popularity of avalanche proportions in the political arena of Ewawa frightened the looters. If they were to perpetrate their diabolic system indefinitely, they had to stop Krudi at all cost. They had to maintain in power the incumbent who had, perhaps without thought, legalized the embezzlement of public funds by asking the population to prove the allegations that his Ministers and close associates were swindlers of state funds.

The elections were a foregone conclusion. Though Krudi would win with a landslide, the Kleptocrats with the backing of France, would rig and deprive him of his victory. So, something had to be done to camouflage the rigging. To make the results look credible, they carried out a whitewashed campaign to impress on election observers (mostly Americans and Europeans who come a day or two before the elections as if elections in Africa are rigged only in polling booths. After watching the ruling party members line up peacefully to vote their man back to power, the observers dash back home the same day or next, with the conclusion that the elections were free, fair and peaceful. But the reality is that only the members of the ruling party are registered. Only they vote. And only they count the votes and declare results. This status quo is maintained with the heavy hand of the police. So, the observers miss every important aspect of the elections and give the world a completely false picture of what takes place) that the ruling clans had had an impeccable campaign machinery and so had won meritoriously. With such dog-licked consciences, such perverse minds, they climbed up to the top of an uncompleted and dilapidating skyscraper abandoned because the funds allocated for its construction had been embezzled by Ministers and contractors) in the city centre, and wrote on all the four walls of its topmost floor, (floor seen all over the city and wrote the election campaign slogan, "Saul Kilcam is the Best Choice". Today, several years after, that eyesore of a skyscraper still carries the slogan like a birthmark, in mute protestation - replicating Ewawians. What a paradox! What a betrayal of the brain power of the leaders of Ewawa! What a husk!

As state institutions and authority collapsed, the masses succumbed to the vicious and incessant lies ERTV (the personalized Ewawa Radio and Television popularly known as Mendomedia) told them, and remained inactive. In fact they remained silent resigning themselves to the philosophy of the poem:

Let's Cup Our Hands To Christ

Though we shrivel in want and move naked,
For the patrons eat theirs and ours,
Though they promise us a golden 'morrow,
A 'morrow that will never come,
Though we can't educate our children,
'Cause theirs must all study abroad,
Though our wives threaten divorce,
Cause we can't provide basic needs,
Let's shut our lips brothers,
Let's cup our hands to Christ.

There's wisdom in shutting lips brothers,
There's insanity in being talkative,
For, shut lips breed peace no matter what type,
Being talkative raises tempers and breeds war.
In peace, able-bodied folk join the begging fraternity
And so ensure even an empty useless life.
But war that's meant to cleanse, never does
It spares the thieves and kills the innocent,
For the thieves possess all the means
To flee to foreign mountain tops,
From where they watch the innocent die below.

So, let's shut our lips brothers
Let's cup our hands to Christ
Let's create a thousand million churches,
 Born Again, Calvary, Apostolic, Revival;
For, thro' them, tho' our fate be sanctioned,
We can turn our nights into days
Consoling ourselves in faith.

But then, that couldn't go on indefinitely. If the grandsons of uncle Marseillaise had reasons to be complacent, the stiff necked grandsons of uncle CNCS could not. They started talking aloud and throwing stones. The police counteracted with grenades and tear gas. In the stalemate, the grandsons of uncle CNCS started doubting whether they were in fact biologically related to the grandsons of uncle Marseillaise. They made blood tests. The tests proved inconclusive. They scanned ethics. There was overwhelming difference. They plied into history. They X-rayed political thought and came to the conclusion that Little John was wrong after all in saying they had some relationship with the grandsons of Marseillaise. For sure, they had no relationship with them. They said history was wrong in saying that their great grandfather and the great grandfather of the grandsons of uncle Marseillaise were identical twins. Wherever they went, they recited the poem,

Jean Bosco, We Are So different

So different in location and history,
 So different in height and bulk,
So different in thought and tongue.
Bosco, we are so different,
So different in body and soul,
So different in mind and heart,
So different in looks and deeds.
Bosco, we are so different,
So different in greed and frugality,
So different in falsehood and honesty,
So different in haste and taste.

So, don't ever call me brother,
Cause we are so different,
So different to be called twins,
So different to be called one.

And even if we were not different,
Even if we were identical twins,
Each of us must have his own wife,
Each of us must build his own home.

As time went on, and Ewawa gradually slipped into a coma, I became most affected by the licensed heartlessness in Ewawa for two reasons. I had to take care of my invalid mother and at the same time, try to save money to lose to the numerous grasping agencies the administration had set up. Ministries launched examinations simply to collect the 10,000 Frs. or 15,000 Frs. examination fees. Such exams were never marked. In cases where they were marked and results published, the courses for which they were meant never opened.

Yet my determination to survive and give my holy family their daily bread still stuck firm in my chest. My country had spited me.

But America, Britain, Germany, France, and all of Europe shone bright with hope. "I shall go to one of those promised lands. Those who laugh last laugh best," I consoled myself and prayed that the God that my father and mother served would help me achieve my aim.

The first sign that God had heard my prayers was my mother's miraculous recovery. She still bore the scarecrow scar-tattoo like an innerwear. But thanks to Medicine without Borders she had recovered the flexibility of most of her body. She could fetch water, cook, and do quite a lot of things she could not do before the arrival of the foreign Doctors who treated her stiff joints. And most of all, she improved everyday.

I was now confident that even if I left her, she would be able to take care of the family. I imagined how the hen that lays the golden eggs in America would be laying in my alms pan and I would be sending some to my holy parents back at home Ewawa, Ewawa that had spited me. Ewawa that belonged more to thieves than to honest citizens. Ewawa that was still my homeland, Ewawa the great. The thought of it all made my heart lose a beat.

To get to America, Britain or any of the promised lands, I had to study hard, really hard to pass an examination and obtain a scholarship. I looked around me. The streets were bustling with thousands of potential candidates for such ventures. But I knew my academic worth. Here Parson, I am not blowing my trumpet. The pocket-clever colleagues who passed the examinations I failed can attest.

Parson, with what I have said so far, can you imagine the strain that had on my body? Do you now see that age may not in fact reflect experience? And that the bullshit the police and the courts insist on identifying a criminal, are matters of colonial status quo? I am sorry, Parson, anger is once more getting the better of me.

I was saying that I knew my academic worth in spite of the thousands of potential candidates for foreign examinations. Most candidates had lost confidence in internal examinations not only because of the extortion and corruption but also because the value of educational institutions had plummeted disgracefully in Ewawa. If people sat external examinations, they sat examinations worth their money. They expected results on individual basis. They knew that the fellows far down or up there in the foreign lands had the human touch and gave their efforts the dignity they deserved. They felt proud of being human beings. But in Ewawa, privileged people passed exams before they sat them and that made nonsense of exams in Ewawa. One saw her examination answer sheets being used to tie doughnuts in front of the Ministries that organized the examination.

So, I became a slave to the American Cultural Centre, the British Council Library and other foreign Embassy Libraries. I felt much more at home with foreign Missions than with the Ministries of my country. The foreign Missions welcomed one with, "Hello, can I help you?" Ewawa Ministries welcomed one with, "C'est quoi? Vous cherchez quoi?" Such repulsiveness and impudence from the owners of my papa's land, sent one's bowels running. One lost confidence in oneself and longed to be something else than being Ewawian. And truly, there were thousands of people like that. People who had divorced themselves from everything Ewawian. People who moved about spiritlessly, who never listened to ERTV (Mendomedia), and who were totally blank of the happenings in the country. The situation worsened with each passing day. But the saddest mistake a disgruntled Ewawian can make is to get discouraged and shy away from the heartlessness of the ruling clans. Once you abandon, they take even what you would have got after a long struggle. I am sorry Parson. I am going out of point again. I see you dozing. Should I say we call it a day for today?

"Lucia, I am really dozing, not because I am tied but because I am imagining the furnace in you. You are an encyclopaedia in Ewawian affairs. But if you won't mind, we can call it a day," he suggested.

"Thank you Parson. If the gods still give me time, we shall see when you next come. But don't forget to take the written document from the guard I talked about if things don't work our way. Good bye.

11

The more I drove toward the genesis of my predicament the more the gall in me surfaced and kept me ill at ease. I feared my intermittent outbursts would make me severe relations with the Parson, who, for Christ's sake, was God sent. But for him, how could I purge myself of the venom that gradually gnawed me to death. If I were to be executed without releasing at least a third of it, I would go to double hells.

The Parson came when I was deep in thoughts. He might have read from the folds of my brows that I was deeply worried.

"Lucia, why today of all days? You should be glad today for I have brought good news. The Canadian Mission with the collaboration of Lawyers without Borders has succeeded in appealing your case. So, rejoice and don't be sad," he said.

"Rev. Parson, I am deeply worried. I am disconcerted by the happenings that have led to my being branded a criminal and sentenced to death, while the real culprits pace the corridors of ravaged Ministries, Parastatals, Banks and Corporations. When I took Geography as my minor, we were taught that Ewawa was rich in all types of products - timber, petroleum, iron ore, diamond, gold, sodium chloride, magnesium, coffee, cocoa, tea, rubber, name it. Yet, these products are getting depleted without the common man even walking on a good road? What has happened? Do you know Parson, that Ewawa is the least developed country in this part of Africa? Do you know that it is only Ewawa that has not yet constructed its section of the Cape to Cairo transcontinental auto route? Why should the citizens of a country overflowing with milk and honey be fleeing from poverty? Why should University graduates become street girls? Why should the population become victim of this organized greed in Ewawa? Parson, to answer these questions most of the people who had hailed the passing away of the old man now hold their tongues. They say, 'You can't compare one thing. It takes two to compare'. The old man had been in power for twenty years (too long for any person's liking) and had become an aching tooth even to the French. The population had wanted it pulled out in the wishful thinking that a new tooth would chew better. As the saying goes, 'It is hell living with a miser, but a bed of roses inheriting his coffers'. And so it was. Kilcam inherited the coffers of the old man. Since a fox doesn't know the cost of a fowl, it eats one with no qualms. Yes, Saul Kilcam inherited the pregnant coffers of the old man. But since he did not know what it took to build them, he unleashed the floodgates of squander mania the old man had put in check. The population saw the delusive phase of things, thought the new tooth was chewing better, went on a praise-singing spree, and led him to chest-pound himself in self-deceit, " Ewawa is waxing on well. I can't go cap in hand to plead for loans from the IMF". Such vain boast did not last. The next day he was seen sprawling, crestfallen at the gates of the IMF, betrayed by his people. In spite of that he still maintained that there was no proof, no proof that his people had raked the nation bare.

Do you know Parson that ever since Saul Kilcam took over, he has created nothing of his own? Has maintained and preserved nothing the old man left behind? Do you know that he has instead lost all, all, all - pregnant coffers, Parastatals like Ewawian Airlines, Ewawian Urban Transport Company, Ewawian Electricity Co-operation, Ewawian Water Co-operation, Ewawian Telephone Co-operation, Ewawian Post Office Savings Bank, Ewawian Produce Marketing Board, Ewawian Stadia, Ewawian Agric Shows and most of all, Ewawian Morality and Unity? Today, after more than two decades of retrogression, the failure of the **New Contract** (Kilcam's catch phrase at take over) has been canonized firstly, in the number of children risking their lives in fleeing the country in high seas and dangerous deserts, and secondly, in the misery and high death rate of the population. But not only the population dies, all flesh is ephemeral. And as this looms threateningly in his eyes, with the bells of his own requiem ringing in diverse forms (in spite of numerous interventions by French and Swiss medical facilities) and fearing that his name might go down in the Guinness Book of Records as the worst leader Black Africa has produced, he now, with the kick of a dying horse, sets the stage once more, this time with another bald expression, **Great Aspirations** - a seven year project to replenish coffers ravaged for twenty four years, and so accumulate funds to fill potholes of battered roads with mud. To do this, the very victims of the **New Contract** must be nailed on the cross and bled to death once more on the stakes of heavy taxes, high cost of petroleum products and the cost of new vehicle number plates. Ewawians are the most heavily taxed people in the world. Ewawa is the only country in the world that is 'fighting' economic crisis by reducing salaries thrice and increasing the prices of all other commodities by more than a hundred percent. Ewawa is the only country in the world that does not audit the managers of financial institutions. Today, Ewawa is a country brooding on a time bomb of tribal hatred. Yet on each nativity, battered Ewawians are persuaded by Mendomedia to sing the nation's hymn and dance their souls to death hailing their doom - replicating the skyscraper. And do you know what, Parson? Eh eh eh, I mean eh, eh... "

"Lucia, I have told you not to be angry today. We have only one thing to do at this time - prepare for your defence. That is all. Leave Ewawa with her problems," he interrupted.

"Parson, if the Ewawian world did not decide to keep quiet, I would not have been in this mess. But because everybody keeps quiet, the plunderers plunder with impunity and create victims of circumstances. Withdraw your appeal. I better die than live to see the realities of our country. It is a shame. Where has our oil money gone to? To import red wine? See neighbouring countries are now discovering their oil reserves and are planning to develop; and in fact are developing, but ours have been sold in advance to provide red wine for the tables of the ruling clans. Please Parson, withdraw your appeal," I said emphatically.

"Lucia, how does what you are saying help us? Why can't we put our heads together to fight your case instead of dwelling on things that don't concern us? If one of the gentlemen with whom I struggled yesterday to have the appeal succeed, heard what you are saying, he would say you are not grateful. Please, shelve your anger and let us work together. Furthermore, what can your anger do to change things? You are just an island in a vast ocean. The anger of a hen cannot prevent the kite from seizing its chicks," the Parson advised."

His advice horned in. He was right. Many revolutionists have been killed and are being killed in Ewawa and though the international community has snarled and is snarling, it has done, and can do nothing. But should the status quo be maintained indefinitely? Should the common man keep paying for the sins of a grabbing management? Questions like these rend my heart. But how helpful can the reaction of a condemned prisoner be? Furthermore, is it not the very crowd that sings hosanna today that shouts crucify him, crucify him tomorrow? The world is in a terrible puddle.

It may be I am under the influence of a type of schizophrenia. This is not the first time it has occurred to me. Whenever I start narrating my predicament and I am about getting to the roots, I develop an escapist's attitude. I start eluding the issue.

"Parson, I am afraid, I want to recompose myself before I go on. In fact, my spirit is willing but my body is weak in my attempt to reveal my predicament. So, give me time. I am extremely nervous now. I may collapse if I continue. Promise me that you will bear with me tomorrow when I tell you the truth of what has robbed me of my honour and that of my family. Even if my pitch rises, bear with me. I shall say it from the bottom of my heart from the beginning to the end. But don't mistake it for a confession. Don't pass any judgement when I am narrating the story; just listen so that you can preserve it when I am dead. My time is short. The executioners may not honour the appeal. They have violated several such appeals before, so, don't be surprised if you come here one day and you don't meet me. Please don't say I am worrying you. Just bear with me. It will soon be over. Thanks," I said.

"OK, Lucia. See you tomorrow. I shall come early," the Parson said and left.

12

"Thank you Parson for coming early. We may not be long. I think the story is not long any more. Since I rehearsed it thoroughly last night, I think I shall not break down. But please pray for us. Lead us in prayers," I said.

In the name of the Father, the Son and the Holy Spirit. Amen. Heavenly Father, Great God, Maker of Heaven and earth, we exalt your name. We call upon your holy name to bless and pity us. Father, we are poor sinners in this vale of tears. Fill us with your holy spirit and sanctify us, so that we may commune with you and praise your holy name to all the comers of the world. Omnipotent, omnipresent God, nothing happens without your expressed will. Father, though the principalities may gather against you, Father you defeat them, for there is no other God but you. Father, before we open our mouths in prayers, you already know what our problems are and how you would solve them. All you require of us is merely to acknowledge your omniscience by channelling our plea through your son Jesus Christ. Father we now channel this pressing problem through him. Lord, be not a judge on us for there is none on all the earth who can stand your justice. Be merciful to Lucia. Solve her problem and the problems of the entire world. We ask this through the loving and saving blood of our Lord Jesus Christ. Amen.

"Thank you Parson though I do not agree with all the prayer," I said and adjusted myself on my wooden bed to brave the oncoming emotionally packed revelations. They may never have the same impact they have on me on any of my listeners, because they may never live my experience.

"Yes Parson, before anger got into our conversation, I was saying that I became a slave to books in foreign Embassies. I read for five hours a day on Mondays and Wednesdays in the British Council Library, five hours a day on Tuesdays and Thursdays in the American Cultural Centre, and on Fridays I went round other Embassies reading the posters at their corridors and reception rooms. Within two months of that self education, my horizon widened considerably. But each passing day brought its own problems in my quest for knowledge. Transport fare from Obele where I lived to the Embassies was six hundred francs a day.

I could not afford it. So I had to trek for five kilo metres to get to the libraries. This meant that I always started studies in fatigue. The libraries had a good supply of water but because of the strict observance of the rules of hygiene, the disposable cups they provided tended to annoy a very thirsty person. After emptying about twenty of the cups, I would sit down to rest before going to the shelves for books. Remember that the trekking did not generate only thirst, it also provoked hunger. The libraries offered water but not food. And of course, you know what that means.

My belt helped me control bowel constrictions. And whenever I plunged myself into the pool of knowledge, only the bell announcing the closing of the library would tell me, "You have read into the night."

Then all hell would break loose, bowels constricting from hunger, distance looming in the eyes, legs creaking from fatigue and courage freezing from fear of former university colleagues turned robbers. Yet, I had to return to the holy family. I still had my natural seal, if at all it remains in place at that age. Holy family ethics did not approve of car lifts even by acquaintances. So, I had to trek. And trek, I did, for several days and weeks and months in the name of the holy family.

One day, was it the day God slept? It may be. My body turned pulpy earlier than expected from accumulated fatigue, and I decided to return. I did not make quite twenty metres from the British Council library entrance. A car pulled up. It homed twice. I did not pay attention to it. I moved on. The car pulled closer and stopped and I heard some one call, "Lucia." I peered into the car, it was Okina Jean-Pierre Marie-Therese, a former classmate I had caught up with in the final year of our degree course. He had passed the ESAM examination on first trial and was now a customs officer. "Hi! Jean, already with a big Mercedes! Congratulations," I said with stabbing jealousy.

"What brings you here?" he asked with pomp.

"Reading at British Council," I responded.

"Still reading at this age?" he asked.

"Yes. To prepare for external examinations," I responded.

"You want to go abroad then," he remarked.

"I have no choice. I have to," I retorted.

"You are just airing yourself out then," he guessed.

"No. I am tired and hungry and so I'm going home," I said without thought. Yes, without thought, like a farting dog.

"Sorry, I would have taken you home but I have to meet a friend at the Ministry of Territorial Administration. If you won't mind, I can drop you at the Central Post Office from where you can find your way home. Come in," he invited and opened the door.

And opened the door of a Mercedes, yes a Mercedes, door of a Mercedes!

I could not resist the temptation. Central Post Office meant my covering a third of the distance. So, I got into the car into a Mercedes for the first time in my life, to be given a lift for the first time in my life, and to appreciate conversing on things other than academics for the first time in my life.

" Massa, this is comfort. Your car is really comfortable," I started the conversation without thought.

"It's an old thing I bought from a departing white customs colleague. My new Mercedes is due in two weeks. If it arrives, my wife will convert this into a kitchen vehicle," he said.

"That is great. You are fine. The customs, the treasury and the taxation officers are in fact swimming in money in this country," I said again without thought.

"So do people think. But these are jobs with no powers.

They are jobs that don't put people in the mainstream of events. No matter the index of one of these officers, a mere District Officer is senior in protocol," he said.

We got to the Central Post Office prematurely. I could not believe that a journey that usually took me forty minutes or more was covered in less than five minutes. When Okina asked, "To which part of the town do you say you are going?" implying that we had reached the Central Post Office and I should step out, I had just begun having the feel of good life - life that mattered. Life we were all craving for in different ways and means. Life which we all had a right to under fair play but life which some of us were being deprived of by I swear to God, this damn set up.

"Obele," I answered in betraying anger. He sensed it. "Then I better take you to the Ministry. It is nearer. You can even propose one hundred to the taxi man," he said and without my consent, drove off.

We met his friend waiting at the veranda of the Ministry. I opened the door to step out.

"No Lucia, don't go out. I better drop you. Obele is not far from here," he said.

"Thank you, but will that not inconvenient your friend?" I asked in pretended sympathy.

"I don't think so. We shall be too early for our rendezvous if we go straight. We'll drop you, then go to where we are going," he said in a big way and invited his friend in. He entered the car at the back and we drove off.

"Joseph-Marie, here is Miss Lucia, a former classmate at the university. Lucia, this is Joseph-Marie Essene, the new Secretary General in the Ministry of Territorial Administration. He was the Director of Customs in the North before his appointment."

"Nice meeting you, Miss Lucia," he said and extended his hand.

"It's a pleasure meeting you," I complemented while shaking his hand.

"Miss Lucia wants to go abroad, probably to Britain, America, or one of those beautiful countries but not France. I met her reading at the British Council," Okina broke the silence after the greetings.

"Why should she go out of her fatherland at this age? To go and read what? To complete when? To return when? To work when? She thinks she can live forever? Life is short and uncertain. There is this wrong conception that those who go abroad are better educated. That is a lie. The value of education is in the pay packet. And by pay packet here I mean, the totality of income, not the indices carried by pay vouchers. It is that totality of income that makes the difference - that makes it possible for some people to start building today and complete the next day and others start building and end up having moss growing on the walls. If I were her I won't waste my time going anywhere," Mr. Joseph advised.

"But what should one do in a country like this? There are no jobs, one can't pass a public examination, one cannot further her studies because the Professors don't teach well, there is total chaos," I retorted.

"Which public examinations did you try?" he asked.

"All. At a very terrible physical and financial cost," I said with bitterness.

"And you could not pass any?" he asked.

"I always passed the written, but lost at the orals. This repeated itself in each of the exams three times. So, I got discouraged and started longing to go abroad. What surprised me is that those who trailed the class at the university were those who passed public exams, but those of us who topped the class at the university failed," I remarked.

"I see. I see your problem. You don't know that there is a difference between an academic examination and a public examination," he remarked.

"What you are saying is very right. Lucia was a very clever girl when we were at the university. We are all shocked that she has not made it into any of these public schools. But since as Secretary General in the Ministry of Territorial Administration, you are in charge of the entrance examination into ESAM, I shall entrust her into your hands," Okina said and pulled up on the curb for me to step out. We had arrived prematurely at Obele where I now had no other choice but to step out. And out, I stepped. But as Okina and Joseph drove off, they drove off with me. In fact, I went down but remained in the car.

I got to our holy family, greeted my holy parents, had my holy seal, was still very much myself, but developed a double conscience. Here Parson, don't mistake me for planning to be wayward. No. I was simply split between continuing my struggle to go abroad, and attempting to take public examinations again, this time with the assurance of an external brain, the S.G. in charge of my previous waterloos.

The SG's argument was tangible. It was six years since I left university. The minor jobs that made money in America and Europe could not be the driving force behind my ambition to go to those countries. I wanted to have a higher qualification and then a good job. But how did this tie in with the time factor. So Parson, I descended from the car but remained in it. Was God awake, was He seeing me, did He know to where I was drifting? Where was my guardian angel?

Parson, can you figure out any scene in what I have so far said that can make you think that I have cause to lie? If I am not lying then don't you think that it is necessary for me to tell the story to the end? I therefore suggest that we adjourn for the day. I have been talking for long. But I have to tell the whole story so that posterity can get the truth rather than police or court tailored facts.

"So, good bye."

"Good bye, Lucia."

As the Parson left, I was numbed with the feeling that he won't come back. I had promised to cut a long story short but every day, the story kept growing longer and longer than I thought. This was perhaps because I kept interlacing it with bouts of anger that led me comment on the ills of the government of Ewawa. Now, was the Parson getting impatient? Will he come back again? I prayed that he should come. Since I could not predict the mood in which he would come, I decided to continue writing. I wrote a few lines but could not continue. So, I surrendered the future to God.

13

The Parson came as he promised. I had rehearsed all night on cutting the story short, but the more I tried the more I found that every iota of it was important. So, I decided to tell him all of it even if we were to be cut short by events.

The next day I did not go to the libraries. I pulled faces at home to the discomfort of my mother who kept asking why I was that depressed. My father as usual spent his time in church cleaning chalices and crucifixes and putting flowers on the altar. An idle day can be very tempting. I thought about Joseph – my father's namesake, and the day the next entrance examination would take place. In my mind's eyes, I saw myself already in ESAM. The fact that our conversation was so down to earth, that is, without strings, made me believe that the encounter was ordained by God. So, whatever emanated from it was God's will. In other words, I was trying to dispel the fear that had been embedded in me that car lifts were dangerous. The worst thing that can happen to a girl is for her to develop double personalities. I was doing so – arguing for, and against my encounter with Okina and Joseph.

The day proved long. The bliss of the car and the hope that I would be helped into ESAM were taking a toll on me, especially as I was now losing interest in the external examinations. For four days, I did not go to the libraries. On the fifth day, I decided to go and see Joseph, the SG. I wanted him to help me have a cleaning job in the Ministry to enable me save money for the oncoming examinations. He received me well but thought a cleaning job in the Ministry for a graduate was too degrading. So he said he would send me to one of the state hotels to supervise the cleaners. On my return, he gave me a ten thousand francs note, still with no strings attached. I thanked him. The salary was pretty good. I could save at least fifty thousand francs a month.

With the acceptance of that job, I severed the exchange of thoughts with my mother. Before that time, we conversed freely on all that concerned me. But in order to make money without bothering them or straining myself as I did in the previous preparations, I left the house in the morning and came back at night. I did not tell her I was working in a hotel. If I had done so, she would have blown up her top. All I needed was money to sit, and be helped to pass the exam into ESAM.

Working in an international hotel is like serving in the devil's temple. I saw terrible things there. Grandfathers came in to have sex with girls as young as their granddaughters. The supposed custodians of our financial institutions squandered state money as if spending money with young girls was developing the country. After three months, I got so disgusted with what I saw in the hotel that I decided to resign. I saw why Ewawa could not develop with the present administrators in place. And linking them with my present predicaments, I hated whatever had connections with them.

But no matter how bad a government is, it is like spittle.

What one can spit out, one spits, what one cannot, one swallows. So I had to thank Joseph for his help although I hated him too for being one of the lioness midwives assigned to assist a delivering goat. I had saved 450,000Frs. from my wages and tips within a few months and I had to be grateful. I went to see Joseph to thank him and to tell him that, though he had overwhelming powers to help me pass, I had to help him also by passing the written part of the examination, and relying on him only in the orals. I did not tell him that working in a hotel was the most obnoxious experience a girl, especially one still carrying her natural seal, could be exposed to.

Joseph was not happy that I said I wanted to put more effort into studies by resigning, instead of combining the two - work and studies.

He asked whether I hadn't confidence in his omnipotence in the examination. I said I did not doubt his powers but feared that anything could happen in the course of time, for example he could be promoted and made Minister of another Ministry, he could fall sick at the time of the examination, or he could go on mission etc. It was therefore necessary for me to pass in the written exam and rely on him only in the orals.

Joseph and I had gone on so well that I could not associate him with evil. For one thing, I always called him dad. I had explained to him that he was my father's namesake. As he bade me good bye, he invited me for lunch at the Parliamentary Hotel the next day. I could not refuse. During the lunch, he made me drink what he called an aperitif - a wine. Food was brought in several courses, and while we ate and drank, (I, drinking for the first time), I thought I was talking and laughing too much. I thought the world was more enjoyable than disgusting. When we finished, I became dizzy and weak. I dangled as I tried to get up. Joseph came to assist me and led me into a room and asked me to take a rest.

When I got up, I discovered some messiness around me.

I had done several bad things. I had messed up the bed, I had thrown up, in fact, I lack words to describe the malaise. In that shame, I cleaned the vomit, bathed and tried to wash the bedding. I did not want to put the cleaners in the embarrassing situation girls usually put us in the hotel in which I had worked. Joseph entered the room without knocking and met me washing the bedding. "Leave that. There are cleaners employed for that. It is late. You have slept for too long," he said and for the first time, to the best of my knowledge, came close for me to kiss him. I refused. I told him that I had never done that in my life and that my kisses and seal were reserved for the person who would marry me. He laughed superficially and patted me on the back. I shrugged my shoulders in disapproval.

He saw me off to Obele junction and I went home. I got home rather muzzy, with a dull headache, undefined thoughts and general listlessness. Something seemed to have gone wrong with me. But what? I could not tell.

The next day, I picked up and started studying for the four public exams. My studies took most of my time. I was so busy that I even forgot about my monthly hoisting of the Russian flag. After registering for the exams, I intensified my studies. I phoned Joseph and told him that I had spent all my savings in registering for the four public exams and I was very busy preparing for them. He congratulated me for always relying on myself. He said he thought he would be the one to pay the fees of the exams. He added that since I did not give him the honour to pay the fees, he wanted to share the burden with me. He wanted to give me 75% of the fees and invited me to come for it and to have lunch with him again.

I don't know what might have happened with me. Was it the shame lunch-taking at the hotel had glued on me; was it the way teenagers were messed up by their granddads? What really uncorked the valve of hatred I had for the plunderers of the economy of my fatherland? I gave Joe a terrible telling off on the phone. I told him I was not one of those girls he could skip around with. I said rather firmly that I did not want his help, that I would pass my exams without help etc. etc. I said I appreciated his help very much but that I, as an Ewawian, had every right too, to the luxury they, the gluttonous clans were enjoying in Ewawa.

That instant insanity put an end to our relationship.

Some weeks to the exam into ESAM, I started doubting whether I had been hoisting my Russian flag at all. Things seemed blurred in my mind. But I had no cause for alarm.

Parson, we have gone perhaps half-way into my odyssey. Do

you find cause for my telling a lie? If not, I think you are now doing the right thing - listening without attempting to comment and passing judgement. Thank you, I believe that the Almighty Father will grant us another session. I am tired and wish to stop.

The Parson breathed in deeply and, thanked me in return.

14

Two days later when the Parson came, he looked withdrawn. I suspected he had fallen victim to the disease of judgement, that is, drawing conclusions from a few panel-beaten facts. I was right.

"Lucia," he called after the normal greetings. "Lucia, the fact that you accepted to work in a hotel makes me feel extremely bad. It makes me believe you got, eh, eh you got yourself, eh, eh ..." he choked in the logic of bad judgement.

"It makes you believe that I got myself messed up. I got engaged in harlotry, or one of those vices," I completed it for him.

"You see, it was dangerous, and I now see where everything went wrong," he said with revamped confidence.

"Now Parson, you have committed one of those sacrileges of judgement that work on my nerves and make me damn the consequences. I damn the consequences by stopping to talk. But in this situation, I don't think sealing lips is the best thing to do. Now, listen. I worked in a hotel in secret in order to make money to register for my examinations without putting undue pressure on my poor parents, or subjecting them to the incessant pain of seeing and pitying me for working myself to death, as they had done in my earlier bids to prepare for the same examinations.

Now Parson, who are those responsible for creating these conditions? Is it God or man? How much do you Parsons pay your catechists? Christ ate with his disciples. How many times have you eaten with your catechist? What should be the fate of the daughter of a catechist or do you call her stone? Do you see any similarities between the church and the state? Do you know that in each case the leaders eat all, depriving even their most fervent subjects? Do you now see why I say you should listen and not comment? Do you know that all mankind is in the mess of greed? Do you now see that you Parsons who rendered my father poor, and those plunderers of state funds, who have caused this devastating economic crisis contributed in sending me to work in the hotel?" I asked with steaming anger, virtually shouting at the Parson.

"OK, Lucia. OK, let's go on with our story," he apologized.

"Parson, I am sorry for that dose of anger. You see, there are things that can alter a person's disposition within a split second. The mere recalling of the events leading to my predicament thrashes my mind with the savagery of the ASP's truncheon. And like all human beings, I tend to resort to revenge. I am sorry that in such cases my anger cannot be controlled," I said in pretended apology.

"I see your point but we should learn to control ourselves.

We should learn to forgive. My interest in this thing is that whether guilty or not, you should reconcile your being with your creator. If that is done, I shall be happy that you will not lose both lives. My remark was not actually a judgement as you took it. It was just a comment, and that is natural in a conversation," he said.

"I understand Parson, but one thing is true, such comments break the speaker's train of thought. However, as you say, let us return to my problem," I remarked.

"Thank you. Let's go on," he said.

"When I abandoned the hotel job and fell out with Joseph, it dawned on me that I had made a mistake in abandoning my ambition to go abroad. It was not yet late. So, I decided to combine courses. The ESAM, ESP, and ESDIR exams required the knowledge of law, while the EHTTS required general knowledge. According to our proverb, 'If one has no walking stick, one should take hold of her knees and plod on'. Joseph or no Joseph, I had to pass the examination into ESAM even if I lost the orals. If I passed and confronted either Joseph or Okina at the orals I would prove my case that entrance examinations into Ewawa job-giving institutions were not objective examinations. They were meant to enrich the already rich, employ brothers and sisters, stock the Civil Service with people of the same ethnic group, and show that Ewawa belonged to some people more than to others.

Get into the ESAM Campus and just watch the fingers of the ladies. Each lady is married, is naturally or artificially light in complexion, is the wife of a Minister, a Secretary General, a Director General, a Banker, a Superintendent of Police, and what have you? And if this status quo is maintained, if girls like me did not through dogged ambition break it, Ewawa would sanction the demarcation of roles. Poor families would remain ever poor. Rulers would remain ever rulers. And that would be it. I refused to accept that as the divine principle. I wanted to break the myth. So I plunged myself into reading, forgetting that I had a body that regulated itself, and whose normal functioning was as important to me, as reading was.

I had begun sharing intimate thoughts with my mother once more. One day, I told her that I was so busy with my exams that I could not remember whether I was flowering or not.

"What!" she exclaimed almost screaming, and thus catching me off-guard.

"I say I can't remember when I last hoisted my Russian flag. There is no cause for concern. I don't see why you are screaming as if frying oil eh, eh, eh." I stammered.

"Whether frying oil or not, there is your father, the Rev.

Parson, the church and the good name of the family. I just don't want to hear," she scoffed.

Brushing her remarks aside, I took my books and went to my room to read. I soon discovered that I could not read. Several things crisscrossed my mind. But how could that be possible. I still had my natural seal, I thought. I tried to make a jack-saw puzzle out of the past. Nothing seemed to lead to any danger. For two weeks, I was subjected to this obnoxious split of personality. I kept arguing for, and against my impossible state. I had no money. I had used up all my hotel savings to register for the exams. I did not want to strain myself again to do a thousand minor jobs to save money. A boil in the mouth is the worst thing. If you want to swallow the pus, close the mouth. If you don't, open the mouth. So, I decided to see a friend very versed in love making but who never got herself messed up as I thought I was. I told her my plight and she suggested I see the doctor immediately. I had to be examined and if it were positive, the age determined, prompt and necessary action would be taken.

My heart took a jolt and almost stopped. Idiot. It can't be positive. Was God alive? Did the Holy Spirit visit me instead of my mother? She was called Maria. I was called Lucy. Nonsense, but I had to see the doctor. See him with what? I had no money. Doctors wanted patients with hard cash and not those who came telling sad stories. I told my friend I had no money. She suggested we go and see her boyfriend - a final year medical student who would be more understanding. We saw him. He examined me for free. He said there were signs of a three months eh, eh, e.

I fainted. When I recovered, I told him I have never had the experience and thought it was a mistake. He then wrote a series of tests I had to do. He said that though he was recommending the tests, he was sure, I was three months pregnant.

"Doctor, what shall I do in this case?" I asked.

"Keep it. It is almost late for any other action. It is risky after three months. The tests will ascertain the age. If it is less than three months, we'll do away with it. If older, you will have to keep it," he said.

"Keep what, an unknown and unwelcome intruder?" I asked with eyes open.

"What is bad in that? You are big enough. If it were the former situation you would have allowances for that. The problem now is this chop-broke-pot situation. Girls shun pregnancy nowadays as if it were a crime. And when they become accidentally pregnant they risk their lives trying to abort. I do help some out, but I am against it. The population of the country is going down because of low birth rate. Boys shun marriage; girls shun childbirth, all because they cannot take care of a family. It's a shame," the medic said.

"What shall I do now? I can't do the tests. I have no money. Doctor, can I wait for a week to be able to work and save money for the tests?" I asked.

"Every passing day worsens the situation. So let me give you a note to take to a friend's clinic. Please, don't disappoint me. If they carry out the tests on credit, make sure you pay them immediately you have money," he said and handed me the note a few minutes later.

My friend and I left at once for the clinic. The results were positive and confirmed that I was three months pregnant. My gall rose into my mouth. I spat what I could and swallowed what I could not. My friend saw that I was in a very bad state of mind. She suggested we see my parents together and tell them the situation.

Her suggestion sounded like a death warrant. If I told my mother, she would want to know the man. Which man? My mind could not settle on Joseph. He was the suspect. But how could he have done it? How do they do it? Neither my education nor my conviction was helpful. I still believed that the doctor and the tests results were wrong.

"Let's go and see the doctor again," I told my friend.

"He will surely say you keep it," she said.

"I think we have to put our heads together. If he reads the results and he says eh, eh, eh," I stammered.

When we got to the medic, he said the tests confirmed his findings. He advised I should keep it.

"But doctor, how can this be possible? I have never had the experience. Can one pick it from seeing other people doing it? Can one pick it by supervising the washing of the bedding on which people do it? Can one pick it by criticizing the people who shamelessly sport it out with their granddaughters?" I asked a million questions.

"One cannot pick it from any of the ways you are enumerating. There should be the real act. You might have been drugged and raped without your knowledge. And that is it. So, face the consequences like a girl of your educational background," the medic said.

His remarks clicked open my mind. Joseph had raped me on the day of the lunch. Joseph, one of them, one of the plunderers of the economy, an ass responsible for the misery of thousands, if not millions of us, had raped me, and now I was pregnant with his child. The world whirled with me. I thought of running to the Ministry and driving a knife through him. I remembered my father's proverb that, 'A spear launched in anger always missed its target.' I decided to lay gins for him by reconciling with him and thereby making him and easy prey.

By the time my friend and I left the doctor, I had not taken a decision on what to do with the pregnancy. But I decided to tell my problem to my parents and the Reverend Parson of the St. John of God's Parish. There was no way I could avoid telling them. Pregnancy cannot be hidden for a long time. So, I had to tell them. I thought starting with the Parson was better. He would understand and cushion the anger of my parents.

15

I had to see our Parson, the Reverend Parson of the Saint John of God's Mission at a convenient time, when he would be more receptive and more understanding. So I chose Saturday evening just after confession. I would go and stand by the corridor of his house and while he returned from the church he would see me and ask me why I was standing there. I would then tell him that I had something very important to discuss with him.

Fortunately that day, the confession session was not long. And on his return from church, only an old woman followed him to his office. He greeted me with a nod and went straight to sell some church relic or so to the woman. Then he invited me in with the preconceived idea that I was once more coming to ask for money to sit exams that I never passed.

"Yeees, Lucia, what can I do for you?" he asked.

"Parson, I have a very serious problem. I shall pray you to help me," I said trying to gather courage.

"Lucia if it is money, I am sorry, I can't help you. The church is going through a financial crisis," he said in the usual way.

"It is not money. It is a personal tragedy. I don't, I can't understand it. I just can't tell what has happened. The doctor says I am pregnant. I cannot believe it but he says it is three months old," I said.

The Parson's brains seemed to have had a jab. He remained silent for a long time, perhaps hallucinating. I thought of continuing but my mind told me to wait for his response. After a while he recovered from the apparent shock.

"Have you told Joseph about it?" he asked.

"No, Parson," I answered.

"What about the man? Does he want to marry you?"

"No, Parson. I don't even know him," I responded.

"That is sad. If you had known him and he was interested in marrying you, I would have been of help. I would have hastened the wedding so that you get married before a scandal unfolds. Now, you say you don't know the person. Were you so perverse Lucia that you don't know the person who impregnated you? I think we have to discuss this with your parents. Joseph and Maria will feel very bad for your letting them down. It will be a terrible scandal. What will the congregation say? What will other denominations say concerning our claim to piety? Lucia, I am

~ 78 ~

shocked. Your father is still in church. Call him," he advised.

I left the Parson's office without calling my father. It may be he called him himself. I went to our house and told my mother what the doctor had said. She leaped into the air, crashed onto the ground and burst out crying. Within a short time my father came in to invite us to the Parson's office. We left immediately and on reaching there, my frowning father said I should tell them what I had told the Parson.

I told them my story from the beginning to the end and gave them the options left. I told them I could risk my life by attempting to terminate the pregnancy. (My mother yelled, calling it murder - the work of the devil incarnate) I told them I could keep it and brave the scandal. (The Parson said I could not stay in the Holy Compound with an illegal and an unsanctified pregnancy.) I said I could leave the Holy Compound and go and live with a friend till the scandal died down. This last suggestion plunged the three into brainstorming. My mother's tears were doubly flowing at this time.

"Joseph," the Parson addressed my father. "Lucia has done a death blow to the good name of this Mission. Wherever she hides, she can't control the scandal.

Abortion is against church teaching. Illegal and unsanctified childbirth is against church teaching. As it stands now, you have to resign your post of catechist and evacuate your compound in the Mission. This will help us control the scandal and also help you help Lucia to deliver her baby. This is the only way out. And we must carry out this as soon as possible so that Lucia's pregnancy is noticed only when you have been well away," the Parson said.

"Parson, Lucia committed her abomination alone. I don't see any reason why I should accompany her to her doom. When Maria and I became Mission workers, we swore that we would serve our Lord till death. I have chosen our burial spots at the Mission burial ground among the saints of this Mission. We shall be buried here and nowhere else. So, we are going nowhere. Lucia must carry her cross, and of course, this night. She shall be driven from this Mission as the angel with the flaming sword, drove Adam and Eve from the Garden of Eden. And when she goes, I shall not want her to use my name or identify herself with me in any form," my father said, stood up and walked out. My mother and I followed him from a distance while the Parson looked on.

"When we got to our house, my father asked me to pack my belonging and vanish into the night. I had little to pack and within a short time I was off to the unknown. My mother watched on as I disappeared into the night. I heard her cry. But she did not call me back. I heard her sob, but she did not run to take me back. I heard her scream, but she did not protest against my braving the night. Yes, my father, my mother and the Parson cast me out of the Holy Mission Compound not minding the dangers of the night, not minding whether I had money or not, not minding my state. Yes, I was illegally pregnant. And of course, the product of an illegal pregnancy was not God's creation. So, I had to go and deliver my unsanctified child in an unsanctified place - the place of skulls.

And so, I Lucia was cast away by my parents and a holy Parson. I had nothing in the form of money. When I was working at the hotel, I bought two new dresses by din of the demand of work rather than the fancy for elegant dressing. The rest of what I carried was my schooldays' old garments. I wandered from compound to compound, from street to street waiting for dawn. It was a long, very long night. At last, dawn came and I had the opportunity to see a friend (Mengue) whose mother was a member of the legion of Mary. I told her about my predicament and asked her to talk to her mother to give me shelter for a few weeks while I looked for means and a place to take care of myself. Mengue Brigitte dutifully told her mother my request and she granted it. I told her my problem and how I came to find myself in the situation I was. She understood and pitied me for being a victim of ignorance.

My health was fine. My determination to survive was unshaken but my mind was not composed enough to prepare for my exams. A few days into my new situation, I heard the exams had taken place. I dismissed the news as a non-event and concentrated on making good my stay with my new found mother. I became a beast of burden. I did most of the laundry, most of the cooking and most of the draining of the marshy compound.

Before long, my foster-mother showed signs she could not live without me. My friend Mengue took advantage of that and time and again, her mother scolded her for giving me her dresses to wash. But as the days passed and the pregnancy developed, I grew weaker and weaker. I started feeling I needed help from a closer relative than a foster-mother. I tended to long for my parents. Although I never went to church, I always asked whether my parents were eager to have me back, whether they ever asked of me. Not one day, did anybody say they ever mentioned me.

My time was drawing near. The medic, my friend's boyfriend had graduated and was now on probation at the hospital. He assisted me the best he could. He even helped pay for the tests I had made on credit. But I could not ask him to prepare me for delivery. He had insisted I should see Joseph and tell him about the pregnancy and ask him to give help. I refused doing so because a man who drugs and rapes a girl cannot be associated with any decency. He was definitely a brute and could take undue advantage of the situation and make his victim more miserable. All around me was misery, but I could not subjugate myself to Joe's dead conscience. So I thought, I could rely on myself and do the best I could in the circumstance. I did minor jobs of laundry and cooking for women who needed such services and saved money to prepare for the arrival of my unwanted baby.

One day, after doing ironing for a long time, the heat from the iron affected me very badly. I felt excruciating pains in my stomach and thought my child had been boiled to death. One lady working with the Ministry of Social Affairs happened to pass by. She saw me wriggling in pains and asked what was wrong with me. I told her my problem and why I did such dangerous work. She was full of pity and advised me to meet her at the Ministry the next day.

The next day, she helped me fill out forms asking for help. I was so grateful. She promised she would follow up my case and make sure I got help from the Ministry. Two weeks later the Minister invited me. She told me that her Ministry had just been split into the Ministry of Social Affairs and that of Women's Affairs. They therefore needed reorganization in order to attribute powers to the different Directorates. She advised me to be patient. She gave me from her pocket, 15,000 Frs. I was so thankful. I went and showed the kind lady the money and told her what the Minister had said. She wished me luck and I departed.

After waiting for two weeks, I went to the Ministry again. I was told to go and wait. I went there six times and was told the same thing six times. While I waited, Directors and Secretaries went on numerous 70,000 Frs. a day missions for ten, fifteen and even twenty days. I could wait but delivery could not wait. I had bought a loincloth, two towels and four napkins. I also had 30,000 Frs. in cash as standby money. I was now getting ready to have my baby. The doctor had prescribed anti-tetanus, some vaccines and other drugs. I thought the standby money was too small to be spent on those items. So, I preserved it. I thought it would be handy if my life was in danger in the course of delivery.

Then my friend suggested that I register in the maternity.

She said, and rightly of course, that though her boyfriend was a gynaecologist he hadn't a maternity where he would deliver me. The maternity of the Central Hospital was virtually a slaughter house. The Ekelimab women delivered there by the minute thus overworking the disgruntled midwives. The place was littered with afterbirth. The stretchers were never cleaned. Sometimes however, people with a conscience who accompanied their loved ones to the maternity cleaned them while the nurses looked on. In spite of those bad conditions, the media recommended delivery in the maternity. So I registered there.

At full term, I went there and delivered my son alone. My foster-mother had gone to the market where she sold vegetables. My friend (Mengue) was nonchalant to accompany me to the maternity when the signs of delivery came. So, I braved it alone. I went and delivered my unsanctified son like a cat.

"You have a boy!" the midwife told me and lifted him up for me to see him. I smiled and got him and kissed him.

"What shall we call him?" she asked.

"Joseph Ntang," I responded, deciding from lame patriotism to name him after my father.

"Were you given anti-tetanus vaccine?" she asked.

"No," I answered.

"What about anti-polio, anti-measles vaccine? Which vaccines had you?" she asked.

"None," I answered.

"We'll need to vaccinate you and the child before we discharge you," she said.

"How much will that cost?" I asked.

"20,000 Frs. officially, but I have the vaccines myself. I shall give them to you for 18,000 Frs. only.

"I don't have money to cover that and maternity charges. So, let's settle for the tetanus vaccine. Anti-polio and anti measles can wait, I said.

"OK, 15,000 Frs.," she said and stretched her hand.

I gave her the money and she administered the vaccine on us. She registered my son, carried out other duties and after four hours discharged me from the maternity. Only women who had problems were kept there overnight, or as long as their problems lasted. Those who delivered safely were asked to make way for other women.

I Lucia carried my child in my hands and my belonging in a carrier bag hanging on my shoulder. I was returning from the maternity alone where I had given birth only four hours earlier. The women who passed me by thought my child was sick and I had carried him to hospital. When one of them sympathized with me in these words, "My daughter, sorry e, e, e, how? Your child is not well?" A numbing sensation ran through me. I broke down and

16

The Parson came the next day much more relaxed than ever. He greeted me cheerfully and told me that the appeal was holding. He added that the Lawyers without Borders were doing everything in their power to stop the secret killings in Ewawa. He said he was confident with the new evidence I was giving, I would be discharged and acquitted.

"Thank you Parson, my main interest is not very much my acquittal. It is the recording of this story as it is. Please, whether I am acquitted or not, you have the obligation to publish my story. I know I can never have the means of publishing it myself. You see, the saints of our society have smeared my name with shit. I am not interested in cleansing it, but I have an obligation toward other victims of our society," I said.

"I have promised I shall record and publish your story," he reaffirmed.

"Thank you Parson. The thought of my parents blurred with time. I had my fate in my hands. First I had to baptize my son on the 8th day of his existence. So, I moved round canvassing for suitable able-bodied men to become his godfather. Of the eight I saw, none had time that day. I saw nine members of the St. Joseph movement. None had time that day. I saw three invalids; none had good dresses to appear in church. So, I went to the place of skulls and four sinners volunteered to be my son's godfather. I chose one and we went to church. The church gave conditions. They wanted to know the father of the child. They asked for church documents (baptism card, church contribution card, etc.) of the would be godfather of my son. They wanted to know whether I was married or not, etc. etc. We could not fulfil these conditions. So the 8th day came and passed and my son was not baptized.

But I went to church with him and prayed for him. I gave him baptism in my heart. After Mass, I decided to go to the Ministry of Social Affairs where my documents for help were. It may be I came rather early. I asked a fruit hawker what time it was. He said it was 10.15am. The doors of the Ministry were still locked. So I thought there was a public holiday. As I was about to move away, a 75,000,000 Frs. Pajero drove in. The occupants got out and one of the boys went and opened the doors. Very soon, another Pajero, of the same make, drove in. The Ministry started filling up. And presently, the sweepers started blaming each other in their native language. Each accused the other of being the person who last had the missing keys. In a mad hurry, they swept the rooms raising dust and sending the workers running away from it. As soon as the dust settled, the workers streamed in and arranged their desks.

I was now sure I would be attended to. So, I moved to the window to which the destitute spoke to the privileged. A beautiful girl soon came and placing her hands on the windowsill surveyed their sphere of influence. From her language, I could determine her level of education. But she was up there and we were down here. The window was three meters higher than where we stood and we had to look up and she had to look down as we spoke to each other. She had a qualification we the beggars hadn't. That qualification cannot be acquired with intelligence, strength or wishful thinking. She belonged to the ruling clan. She was the daughter of the soil. And that made the difference. We could go hang if that did not please us.

"Madam, you people should go and come tomorrow. The Minister is occupied today," she said.

"Just dismiss us for good and don't say the Minister is busy. We have heard that several times. What is the Minister doing that prevents her from seeing the needy for whom she was appointed?" a nursing mother said angrily over my left shoulder.

'They say the Minister is receiving the contractor who won the 1,350,000,000 Frs. contract to build a fence round the Ministry of Social Affairs. After that they will have a party given by the contractor. Since he is a brother of the Minister, the party will spill over to the village. So we better go. What can we do?' an elderly woman on crutches shouted with drawn brows.

"Why has this present leadership specialized in fence-building? Every Ministry is enclosed in a mammoth fence perhaps to ward off thieves. But so long as I know, this nation is plundered on paper (transfers of state funds to foreign bank accounts abroad) and not through break-ins. Each Minister engages his company in the fence-building business to make money for themselves. See, the road leading to the Ministry of Public Works is virtually impassable because of deep craters. Yet, the Minister is engaged in building a mammoth 1,500,000.000 Frs. fence rather than repair the road. I hate the attitude of these Ministers toward public utilities. The shame of it all is that even the Ministry of Social Affairs in a destitute country like this, is engaged in that foul business, and that of buying Pajeros from Japan. It is said that Doctors without Borders donated vaccines to the tune of 50,000,000 Frs. In response to this, or better still, in appreciation and show of good faith, the Ministry of Health in collaboration with the Ministry of Social Affairs spent 500,000,000 Frs. to buy Pajeros for the distribution of the vaccines throughout the country. What patriotism! What magnanimity! Ewawa o bosso.'

"You are taking it lightly. But let me tell you, fences cannot make a capital city beautiful. If you are in the air, our fenced Ministries look like leprosy settlements. In reality, each fence is a fief of robbery," a middle aged woman who had returned from France for treatment remarked.

"You see, our leaders should learn to treat us with even a minimal degree of respect. This is the 20th time I have come here to ask for help for my invalid daughter. I only want specially made lightweight crutches the Minister herself told the nation were donated by Japan for children below six years of age.

But it seems as if the speech she made when she was receiving the gifts from the donor country was mere window dressing. This is of course, standard practice. If you go to hospital, they tell you there are no vaccines in the hospital pharmacy. They tell you there are no free vaccines. But the other day when the Minister of Health was receiving tons and tons of vaccines from UNICEF, he said Ewawian children in the rural areas were henceforth going to be vaccinated free of charge. Today, the vaccines have ended up in the hands of the nurses who sell them at exorbitant prices in urban hospitals. It is even said that the drugs in the hospital pharmacy belong to private individuals who buy donated drugs from the Minister at wholesale prices and retail them in the hospital pharmacy. Instead of telling us the truth, they keep making us nurse hopes and make us come and line up here waiting for godot," my former classmate said. She too had had an unwanted baby and was lining up to ask for help from the owners of papa's land.

At this time the line of women on charity had extended across the road. My son started agitating. I expected it. The fellow was a voracious eater. I breast-fed him out of necessity and not out of the merits of breast-feeding our media deafened our ears with. I never breast-fed him in the open. I was still very shy to expose my breasts in public. So, I withdrew from the window and returned to feed my unsanctified child at home.

"Lucia, I would have preferred you to discuss what concerns you instead of discussing a gamut of other people's grievances," the Parson broke his silence.

"Yes Parson. But we cannot dismiss the we-ness of my situation. And that is why I say that this story be preserved as it is. It is a story in which 'I' cannot be distinguished from 'we'. When I was going to the Ministry of Social Affairs, it did not occur to me that I would meet women with problems like mine. I thought mine was a unique case. But see, we are in the thousands if not in the millions. If the story is too long or if you are tired we can call it a day today too. I am sorry but I can't cut the story shorter than what I am doing now. Thank you." I said.

The Parson was visibly tired and so he promised he would come the next day.

17

I was glad the Parson came three days after our last encounter. He might have lost enthusiasm in the story. But because he believed we were nearing the end, he came convinced that I would be brief. He greeted me with restrained cordiality. I responded rather casually too. In that mood, both of us had to put flesh into our task in order to make it worthwhile.

"Reverend Parson," I addressed him. "I thank you for all that you have sacrificed for me. I think we shall end our story today and give the executioners their leeway. I am particularly thankful to God for enabling me narrate this story to the end. You would remember that last time we ended when I left the Ministry to go and breast-feed my son at home. Nothing specific happened after that. However, we kept making futile trips to the Ministry. When my son was one year old, I noticed that he was the carbon copy of my father. At first, I felt a type of nondescript guilt in me. I asked my foster-mother why my son resembled my father. She explained that my father resembled his grandfather and it was his grandfather who had come back to me to be born again in the family.

That explanation did not please me. So, I went and asked the Doctor. He talked about genes and all what not. However, I thought if my father saw a re-enacted self in my son, he would be excited and reconcile with me. So, on Sunday, I asked my foster mother to carry the child to their church and show the child to my father and mother. She returned with negative reaction from both of them.

In spite of that, I did not lose hope. I was told the scandal was dying down. People hardly discussed it anymore after mass. According to my foster-mother, some women showed a lot of interest in the child and chided my parents for being so hardhearted. So long as I was concerned, I was condemned to love the child, to fend for him and to protect him. Legal or illegal, he was my child. Whether I liked it or not, I had to bear him as a cow bears its hump - the curse of being woman. Thank God he did not resemble his biological father. If he had, it would have been a constant stabbing reminder of that awful hotel lunch-taking experience with Joseph, and that would have perhaps affected my disposition toward him.

One day, he fell seriously ill. All the symptoms showed that he had malaria fever, especially as we lived in a mosquito infested area. I rushed him to hospital. After queuing up for hours I was asked to do a series of tests for him. This meant that the child would stay untreated for another day or so, since I had to look for money for the tests. I did not consider it wise for me to carry back the child without buying some malaria drugs for him. So, I decided to buy whatever drug, roadside drug hawkers (the doctors and pharmacists of the poor) would recommend.

The prescription was automatic. There was no consultation fee. There was no queuing up for hours. There were no impudent nurses there to usher in their late-coming relatives to see the Doctor before the people who had been queuing up for hours. There was no spiting of the patient. All that to me was the human touch, the we-feeling that did not exist in our hospitals. Furthermore, the drugs were cheap and effective.

The next morning, my son was on his feet. That was what mattered: not beautiful and air conditioned premises with perfumed interiors, and stacks and stacks of medicines ostentatiously displayed on glass shelves; not glass counters behind which gorgeously dressed-in-white-apron over creamed pompous damsels, with thick eyeglasses, lifted up their noses (to hold the glasses in place) to read doctors' prescriptions and then start dragging their feet on the floor as they moved to the shelves to get the medicines; not the ritual of moving up to the computer-lady to pay for the drugs, and she would place the balance on a glass tray for one to struggle to pick up the coins from the smooth surface of the tray. And of course; not even the well painted or marbled exteriors of the premises with sophisticated neon lights beaming, advertising the Pharmacy and its Paris ¬trained pharmacist whose Paris lifestyle had to be sustained with the high cost of the drugs. Yes, it was not at all, that repulsive and arrogant display of discriminatory beauty that mattered. It was the effectiveness of drugs no matter where and by whom they were sold. The display of beauty, with its consequence of high prices (death warrant for the poor) cows our simple souls to death and fills us with hate. Many more people die everyday by the careless hands of Ewawian Doctors and nurses than by wrong roadside prescriptions and expired drugs sold by self-employed outcasts of our society. Yes, that display of beauty, as if being sick is beautiful, drew the line of demarcation between the sanctioned to live and the sanctioned to die in Ewawa. The cars of the former line up in front of pharmacies, the rags of the latter litter the fronts of roadside medicine shacks.

Now, who's responsible for that mess? - a government that can't provide essential drugs and vaccines to hospitals? Poorly paid and disgruntled Doctors and nurses who defy medical ethics by carrying out the policy of 'work as you earn'? Doctors and nurses who in reaction to poor working conditions steal all the drugs donated to hospitals? Doctors and nurses who lure patients from government hospitals to their private clinics where they finally kill them? Extortive drug prices in pharmacies for the upkeep of the pharmacists and their teams of employees (mostly relatives) and the sustenance of the French economy? Or, the actors (roadside doctors and patients) in this 'jam pass die' (hunger is worse than death) situation created by a heartless setup? The plain truth is that, a Government that has nothing to offer strives on trivialities to divert attention from its failures. Yes, after treating my son with the roadside drug, he got well. He got well. Yes, he got well, and that was what mattered.

The very day my son got well, Ewawian TV showed in the evening, the destruction of tons and tons of roadside drugs the gallant Ewawian police and gendarmes had captured from hawkers - most of them graduates turned hawkers. The Divisional Officer in charge of the zone was awarded a medal for the capture of the drugs. The pharmacists of the zone threw parties for the capture and destruction of the drugs. The Doctors of the zone held state sponsored seminars on the dangers and disadvantages of roadside drugs. The party in power (The Ewawian Progressive Party for Advanced Democracy) was hailed for a job well done. The French Ambassador phoned to congratulate the Head of State for his magnanimity and promised that France would provide him with helicopters to police Ewawian borders with neighbouring countries, especially Biberia. The ruling party gave the Head of State a vote of confidence and promised him a renewable twenty year term of office and if death caught up with him, the pledge would be given to his son to rid the nation of illegal drugs, and to further lead the nation to greater prosperity. The Presidential Majority Youth Wing of the party (radio and television made Youth Wing) held demonstrations all over the national territory in support of the Head of State and called on him to deal mercilessly with smugglers and hawkers whose aim was to destroy the economy of our dear motherland and tarnish her image abroad.

In his magnanimity, the Head of State declared a two-day public holiday to the nation and instituted another special risk allowance for all law enforcement units in the nation. He further decorated the heads of the Police, Gendarmerie, and Military. To crown his satisfaction at the progress of the country, he took a three-month leave with his family and his children's teachers and their families to Switzerland.

Elated by these happenings, University students of the First, Second and Third Provinces formed vigilant groups to counter opposition propaganda. The fight against drug trafficking intensified. Drugs prices skyrocketed in pharmacies. Doctors in government hospitals signed pacts with pharmacists. They prescribed drugs and sent patients to specific pharmacies. And the next consultation or treatment was done on condition that the patient showed proof of having honoured the previous engagement by showing the receipt given by the pharmacist.

Pharmacists now enjoyed the monopoly of the drug trade.

The rich bought the drugs with ease. The poor eyed them on pharmacy shelves. The police, the gendarmes and the military watched the two groups live with diseases and drug prices. The death rate increased five folds in the national territory. Mendomedia sang the praises of the regime. Life went on in Ewawa, our dear, very dear papa's land. Ewawa was acclaimed the most peaceful country in the world although every street man was an abscess full of the puss of hate. Peace and tranquillity reigned, so to speak. Parson, I am rather tensed up. I am afraid I shall collapse. Please, I need a short break. My head is throbbing. My throat is dry. I need to cool down. It's horrible. Wha, wha, shii, !

18

I thanked the Parson for his patience, especially as he never interrupted the story. Although I knew that passive listening could lead to absentmindedness I did not like him to interrupt by making comments or asking questions. I feared either of those two actions would inflame me and disrupt my train of thought. Fortunately he understood and bore with me. Yes he bore with me because he too bore witness to what was going on in Ewawa. Although the world acclaimed Ewawa as the most peaceful country in the world, they knew that Ewawians had just resigned themselves to their fate.

Parson, another phase of my predicament started soon after the capture and destruction of the drugs. Ewawa was in a state of siege with the vigilant groups terrorizing the common man in the day, and armed robbers, in the night. Since our gallant Ewawian troupes (police, gendarme and military) operated in both camps, the common man was wedged between them. Life became unbearable. The Government announced an increase in oil prices. The prices of other commodities skyrocketed. Insecurity at night affected the buyam-sellam trade, or buy and sell trade which was the main stay of my foster-mother.

When there was security, she left the house at three o'clock in the morning for the market. There, she bought vegetables and other food items from village women at wholesale prices and retailed the things in the day. And from the proceeds of her trade she fed us. But as insecurity set in, she could no longer leave the house early in the morning. Feeding us became cumbersome and she started agitating. Furthermore, my son had started wandering from the house and playing in the marsh and like most other children was eating dirt. He thus became a constant victim of diarrhoea and related diseases prevalent in the slumps.

There is nothing as nauseating as the diarrhoeal droppings and vomit of a non-relative's child. My son's illness made him cry and disturb us constantly at night. The shrill cry of a sick child at night can be very annoying to a person whose sleep is preciously programmed. Over the years, my foster-mother had programmed her sleep. And if anything disturbed her from sleeping at specific hours, she became snappish and waspish, and would cluck for minutes on end. Sometimes I pitied her as I feared she would sore her throat with the clucking. Under such conditions, I longed for a person closer to me than a foster-mother. And yes, I was right. My relationship with my foster-mother started creaking like a snapping tree branch. Her nagging and clucking and sometimes downright scolding of my sick child filled my heart with 'chirping chickens'. Time and again, she made remarks from which I could infer that she wanted me to return to my holy parents. As such, I found myself in a situation akin to that of a hare thrown in a cage with a sleeping python.

I saw the monster gradually coming to life. Parson, I saw the monster gradually getting poised for action. I had to avoid it. And the only way was by either temporarily or permanently leaving my foster-family. I may be wrong in my analogy. I may be impolite or downright impudent to allude to such a wonderful and benevolent woman as a python. But, Parson, what I saw as a sleeping python was the way our relationship was incubating a quarrel between us. An apology is like a scar. It may not hurt but it is always a stabbing reminder of its origins. Yes, and whenever it reminds one of its origins, it creates one's mood and disposition to relate with the other that day. I did not want a situation that would lead to either my apologizing or my foster-mother apologizing to me after a quarrel. That would ruin all I owed her. I had held her in very high esteem. So, I thought prompt action, no matter how unwise and risky it was, was necessary.

One evening, I told her that I wanted to visit my cousin married in a village 60km from Dande. I said I would leave the next morning: and would be there for about a month or two. She asked whether my child's clothes were clean, whether my cousin was informed, and whether I knew the place very well. I said all was OK. In her usual kindness she prepared me some egusi cake, some miondo, and gave my child the napkins she had thought of giving him upon my mother coming to take me. When I was leaving in the morning she gave me 3,000 Frs. for my fare and pocket money. I used part of the money in buying bread and sardine for my friend. I then left for the 'unknown'.

I headed for a village called Etambeng, the village of a former classmate at the University. I did not inform her I was coming but I was confident I would meet either her or one of her relatives in the market in an adjacent village. The market held on Thursdays and most people of neighbouring villages attended it. We arrived at the market at 11.30 a.m. after a four hour fifteen minutes gruesome ride interlaced with six police checks, fifteen minutes long each.

The last checkpoint remains indelible in me. We had not done up to five minutes from the second to the last checkpoint when our driver bumped into a barricade freshly and crudely mounted at a blind comer at the crest of a hill.

"Frieeeeeeiiieeeiiieee!" the police whistle sounded. Our driver stopped instantaneously.

"Stupid!" he insulted. "They are never here. This place is extremely dangerous. Look at the treacherous gorges at both sides of the road! This is a ridge and not a road. Any oncoming vehicle on average speed would bump into us at this place," the driver remarked angrily.

"And we'll go tumbling down the gorge," a passenger complemented loudly, not minding whether the police would hear the remarks and charge him of treason.

"What the hell! What bad luck!" another passenger exclaimed as he saw the police emerge from a thicket,

From every indication, the two policemen who had stopped us were in for some sort of clandestine business. There was no reason why in the name of goodness, the police from the same police station would mount two control checkpoints less than a kilometre apart in thick forest.

"Pierce!" the first policeman ordered and stretched out his hand to take the documents.

The driver handed him the documents with confidence. He examined them with the curiosity of a fox and grimaced in surprise. The driver had all the documents - carte grise, vignette, insurance, a receipt showing that he was in the process of acquiring the new number plate, driving licence, park charges receipt and bordereau. In addition, he had a First Aid box well protected in a carton. The police opened the box and were astonished by its contents. Unlike what they were used to, medication for fresh wounds and blisters, necessary First Aid implements like blades and splints were there.

"Pierce personnel!" the disappointed policeman ordered. The driver handed him his identity card and tax receipt. The police examined them over and over again. He swallowed hard and handed the documents to his colleague. He too went in for thorough scrutiny of the documents. He squirmed around in disappointment. He shook his head several times in contemplation, and tended to say that having all documents was not good enough for the driver to go scot-free. No, he hadn't, he hadn't to go without bribing his way through with at least 500 Frs. If every driver had all documents, would the police 'eat' documents? Bullshit, all documents or not, the driver had to pay for daring to use the road - a police exclusive facility.

"Certificat de visite technique," the first policeman (ASP)

bellowed. Our driver looked confused - totally crestfallen. He had never heard of that.

"Visite technique c'est quoi?" the driver asked with a trembling voice. At this, the police were jubilant. They had got their man at last. The driver hadn't a road worthiness certificate for his vehicle. And so, he was in for it. The police were now sure they would squeeze from him half of what it cost to do a certificate of road worthiness for the vehicle. Since no other person knew what it cost, whatever they charged, the driver would have to pay.

"Descendez" the police thundered as rejuvenated confidence and the thought of making real cash raced in their brains.

"Descendez," they ordered in unison, their hands trembling in demonstrating what they meant. We traded glances of shock at each other. Our arching joints creaked as we rustled to obey.

"Don't go down!" a voice cackled from a reticent, sullen and diminutive fellow sitting by my side.

I looked at him in derision. I felt hatred for him swell in my brains as I thought he was worsening our situation by being so impudent to the almighty policemen - the alphas and the omegas of Ewawa. One lady tried to go down.

"I have told you madam not to go down. Enough is enough," the fellow decreed in an authoritative, convincing and powerful voice. But his build did not match his voice and so we smiled at the folly. To prove that he meant what he said, he got up and stepped out and confronted the police.

"Officers, what do you say you want?" he asked in a low but very reassuring voice. The police eyed him disdainfully, the way one spites a leper. He moved close to the ASP in a more imposing and self-assertive manner and asked him once more what they wanted. The ASP replied that they wanted the road worthiness certificate of the vehicle. If the driver hadn't it the vehicle won't be allowed to go. The diminutive fellow burst into guffaws to the embarrassment of the police and us.

"Can you show me 'le certificat de visite technique' of this road? Tell me officer, has this road undergone any technical studies and found fit for vehicles? Has a caterpillar ever passed through this road, not to talk of working on it since the old man's death? Is this road vehicle worthy? If the road is not vehicle worthy, how can you expect the vehicle to be road worthy? Look, put yourself in my place. I went to Dande in my car. I am coming back without it because this road ruined it. I have abandoned it in a garage. If I am not careful, I may lose it. The longer it stays in the garage, the more the garage boys steal its parts. So, whether vehicles are road worthy or not, so long as the roads are not vehicle worthy, the equation is the same. Furthermore, why should your thinking always be one-way thinking - thinking that is aimed at blaming the ordinary citizen with the foul aim of exploiting him? The people who sent you to ask for certificates of vehicle road worthiness should have told you that they have not carried out their own part of the obligation," the fellow said, his stony face twitching probably from anger.

He re-entered the vehicle and ordered the driver to go. The driver smiled at the joke. If he obeyed, he would be putting his future use of the road in jeopardy. The fellow got down again and asked the two policemen to move out of earshot from us. He apparently introduced himself to them. We saw him show them what appeared to be his identification papers. The police at once gave him military salute. He came back in a rather subdued manner and sat down again.

"Chauffeur, allez y avec patron," the police said and bade us good-bye.

We batted eyes at each other and swallowed hard in admiring our David. We all doubted why he had not used his powers in the other police checkpoints. We tried to make him talk, to introduce himself to us, but he kept quiet. In being quiet, we admired him the more. A tingling glow of love and respect for the fellow raced through me. I eyed him admiringly and thought that one day, it would perhaps not be size and might that would save Ewawa from the stranglehold of this regime but meekness and simplicity. Fifteen minutes later, the vehicle wheeled onto the sidewalk. We sighed in anger, thinking we were in again for another police check.

"En fin" a passenger exulted. We had arrived! As we alighted from the vehicle, we shook our heads and thanked God that at last, the rocking and bouncing and bashing, and all what not, have come to an end.

We were all covered with dust. After tidying up my son and myself I looked for a strategic position where I could easily see my friend. Twice, a girl passed by and tended to look at me closely. I also looked at her with keen interest. On the third occasion, she called "Lucia," in a very low and trying-out voice. I answered expectantly. She jumped at me and started hugging me. I hugged her in return.

"Lucia, what has brought you here? How are you? Married and with a child already? How are you?" she asked a thousand questions and took the child from me. She kissed him tenderly and asked his name.

"Joseph," I answered.

"Joseph, welcome. Welcome Joseph. How is your dad? How is Dande the capital city of Ewawa? City people have come to the forest. Welcome," she said, still hugging the child.

My son who usually detested strangers remained calm in my friend's embrace.

"That's funny. Joseph avoids people he doesn't know; but he behaves with you as if you have lived with him for long," I remarked.

"Yes, blood is thicker than water. The other people are strangers, I am his mother," Jeanne joked, really elated.

"Lucia Ntang," she called.

"Jeanne Olembe," I called back.

"Lucia Ntang," she called again, and jumped at me.

"Jeanne Olembe," I called back again.

Something seemed to be missing in that exchange. Each of us tended to be holding back something - the reason why we could not recognize each other at first sight. Jeanne, a once pearl of average beauty at the university had been reduced to a skeleton by village hardship. And I, now bearing the badge of motherhood, might have withered beyond recognition. At the university, we had one thing in common, boys referred to us as the Marys, the strict girls.

"What do I do with you now, Lucia?" she asked.

"What you want to," I responded.

"We are going to my house then?" she requested.

"Yes," I responded.

"Let's go," she ordered, and carrying my son, led the way to where she had kept her things. She made three bundles out of her things and what I had and asked some children to help carry them to Etambeng about 2 kms away.

We were the first to reach the village. Upon arrival I was shocked at the look of the village only 60km from Dande the capital city of Ewawa. The village had not changed for the better ever since my last visit some six years earlier. In fact, it had deteriorated instead. The buildings were in very poor shape. There wasn't much difference between those with corrugated iron roofs and those with thatched roofs. The former had, because of poor material texture, been corroded and perforated to a point where they looked like graters. And the latter had been so badly eaten by weevils and termites that they were virtually transparent.

The mud walls were caving in and collapsing in some places. I couldn't believe human beings lived in them. But very soon, smoke started billowing from the buildings with the return of the village women from the market. The men dressed mainly in second hand pantaloons and bare footed, remained behind to empty the bars along the road from the marketplace to their respective compounds.

Parson, you may consider this part of the story irrelevant. But let me tell you, every part of the story I tell you is worthy of note because it throws more light on 'The Day God Blinked'. 'The Day God Blinked', is neither mentioned in the Bible nor does any church tradition make mention of it. So, it needs greater explanation. I need to go into minute details to give the gist of it. I am saying this because you are making faces as if you do not want me to talk about my impromptu visit to my classmate, a graduate turned a suffering village girl.

"Yes, Lucia," he broke his silence. "I don't very much see where God blinked in the whole situation. Your story is pathetic but every turn of it seems to show more of human folly than God's. So there are two things you need to convince me about their relevance, your referring to being a woman as this cursed thing called being a woman, and your insistence that God blinked."

"Thank you Parson," I responded. "This story is for people who can draw inferences from a story. That is why I say, every iota of it is important. Since we are tired today and the appeal is holding, I pray that we adjourn for the day."

"Yes, Lucia I shall see you tomorrow," he concluded and left.

19

The Parson came the next day and told me to skip the village experience and go on with the story. I told him I could not because the village experience was the Gethsemane of the story. It was imperative for me to tell the whole story.

"OK, go on," he encouraged.

"Thank you Parson. As soon as we arrived the village, Jeanne carried my things into her room and quickly arranged the bed for my son and me. Then she got a large piece of the bark of a tree and laid it on the floor on the left side of the room. She spread dry plantain leaves on it, covered them with an empty raffia bag, then spread a loincloth on it. That was to be her bed. Apart from the raised platform, there wasn't much difference between that arrangement and my bed. After the delicious evening meal (for she welcomed me with a well prepared rooster) we went to the room. We sat on the bed and eyed each other for some time before she broke the silence.

"Lucia, thank you for coming to see me. I wonder how Dande looks like now. I have not been there for three years. The fare is prohibitive. Prices have skyrocketed and so we take refuge here in our forest," she said.

"Dande is OK to those who own it. Paupers have it rough," I responded.

"How is your husband - Joe's father? Sometimes water is thicker than blood. You got married without inviting me. And even when you begot your child, you did not think of informing me. Wa, wa!" she exclaimed with a smack.

My ears hummed in confusion. Several lies raced in my mind.

"He is well. He left last week for the UK for a two year study leave. Being miserable, I decided to visit you," I lied.

"Congratulations," she responded, and added from apparent jealousy induced spattering that she had been trying to woo a primary school teacher there to take her for free, but whenever they met he talked of 'tisam', premarital sex.

"I tell him there is no 'tisam' until the consummation of the deal. This time he does not even come."

"A primary school teacher! For a graduate! Anyway, Susan Etando is married to a police constable a class seven fellow. You see what we have become! Men now carry their shoulders high, very high and make a mockery of us because the woman is the worse hit in any crisis. Joblessness and hardship have driven especially the heartless girls into stooping to them. The worse of it all is 'bush-falling' - going to Europe to harlot." I taunted.

"What can we do? What about Susan Besem, Etioline Epede, and Solange Ebanda, the light in complexion girls of our class?" she asked.

"I believe they are all well. They all got married. Susan got married to the son of the Minister of Public Service, Etioline to the Director of Ewawa People's Bank and Solange to the Secretary General of Dande Urban Council. I hear even Fegolina Nzama who nearly lost her eye in a fight with the former wife of the Director of Public Works got married to him soon after returning for treatment from France. I knew the poor woman was fighting a losing battle. I wonder why she thought she could contest a husband with the descendant of a Greek merchant," I responded.

"She was not contesting. She was trying to protect her marriage. Which woman would get married nowadays and allow an intruder to deprive her of her man? I would have done the same thing. You would have done the same thing. She knew she would lose her husband to a mulatto and that is why she went in for the kill. Before the fight, she had warned Fegolina to stop running around with her husband or else she would beat her and make her look like the victim of a fatal accident. And when it happened, it was terrible. But for good medical intervention, Fegolina would have lost her eye. God bless her," she remarked.

"Really God has blessed her. But who knows? The enemy never sleeps. I am convinced Madam is still planning to deal with her. I hear Fegolina does not go anywhere nowadays without an escort, a bodyguard." I said.

"What has she seen? She has imprisoned herself, and she is not the type that would like to be under surveillance," she said.

"I believe that will help keep their marriage. The Director is a pretty ugly man, and he himself knows that Fegolina does not love him. While we were at the University, he maintained their relationship only by dishing out large sums of money to her. Most of the loose girls of our class are married but the strict ones are sweeping the streets." I remarked

"What a reversal of values! Aren't you lucky!" she exclaimed.

The house whirled with me. I could not hide the reality about my situation anymore. I told her at once that I was not married after all, that I was the mother of an illegal child, and the circumstances under which I bore him, and the raison d'être of my visit. She gasped but made no hurting remarks.

Our conversation went on and on. Although we ran out of kerosene, the moon was merciful. Its rays lit the room through the amazing network of perforation in the roof - giving a chequered outlook reminiscent of a night-club-lighting in a hotel. It seems we had dozed off by early morning for we were woken in the late morning by my son's screams.

I needed water to wash his napkins. My friend offered to fetch some. I accompanied her to the virtually dry ravine at the bottom of which the villagers had made a mud dam to hold back the little water that dripped from a rock. The place was heavily trampled but there seemed to have been order.

My friend descended to the pool and beat the surface of the water with her cup to dispel the spawn and moss that had laced its top. When most of it had drifted to the sides, she scooped several cupfuls and filled my bucket. She repeated the operation and filled hers too and we returned to the house. As the water settled I realized that we had carried quite a handful of tadpoles and moss. I picked them up with my hands to clean the water and then washed my child's dirty napkins.

"Jeanne, what happened with the water project of this village? I remember when we came here on weekend when we were at the university, there was a water project going on in this village," I enquired with great concern.

"After the death of the old man, all the projects he left behind were considered archaic and so discontinued. The new government talked of buying new equipment and having the pipes laid by a Paris trained engineer who would build self-filtering tanks. You see, the old pipes are abandoned. The water points are collapsing and it is believed the contractor with the complicity of the Divisional Officer had received all the funds for the contract. So, all is dead. Last year by this time, there was a terrible cholera epidemic. We lost half the child population in this village.

This village is blessed with a good water source, one that does not dry up even in the most severe dry season. The neighbouring villages are worse off. At the heart of the dry season, some of their people migrate to far off villages. Those who remain behind fell plantains and bore holes into the stumps. In the morning, they collect the water that had accumulated in the holes overnight. Lazy ones collect dew very early in the morning by putting containers under foliage heavy with dew, and beating the foliage with their palms making the dew drain into the containers. That is mostly done by women and very young children. Sometimes there is no foliage at all, especially when every leaf dries up in a severe dry season.

We have tried to advise the men to rely on themselves and form groups to dig wells. But they spend most of their time drinking and believing in the lies politicians tell them on the eve of Election Day.

When they had good cocoa harvest and prices were good, they squandered their money in bars. And of course, since the death of the old man, there is a bar in every house by the roadside. Today, the men can't even repair their dilapidating buildings. They are broke to the bone when it comes to replacing corrugated iron or thatch on the roofs. But when it comes to drinking and telling tall stories about the virtues of the ruling party and the so-called great men of Ewawa, they chest-pound themselves as if that would make them too great." she explained.

I was horribly shocked when I heard a university graduate call a mud pool (breeding ground for amoeba) good water source in comparison with the water sources of other villages, villages of the ruling clans - villages less than a 100km from the capital of Ewawa. And of course, there are villages 1000km from Dande, if not more.

"Jeanne, it seems this area hasn't great sons and daughters in government. I don't see beautiful buildings around and no development projects going on. Even the neighbouring villages don't seem to fare better. Old and dilapidating German buildings suggest that Otang was a very important commercial township," I remarked.

"Our big men build in modern townships - in Dande, Tuada, Kilbi and so on. Whenever there is a development meeting of this area, they prefer to drive from their respective townships and come early in the morning for fear of witchcraft. They never pass the night here. There is a development meeting on Sunday. We shall attend it and you will see the types of personalities we have here. They will come early in the morning, they will bring their food along, they will bring mineral water and canned beer and soft drinks which need no glasses, or if at all they need glasses, they bring them. They don't share containers of food and drinks with the natives for fear they would be poisoned by the natives," she explained.

"Then what is the purpose of development meetings? Is it to discriminate against their disadvantaged kith and kin? What, if one of them dies? Do they bury him in Dande? What do they discuss in the development meetings?" I asked really concerned.

"The last meeting ended in a terrible tumult. Nothing tangible was discussed. The chairperson who is aspiring to be a member of Parliament spent all the time trying to woo back the people to the ruling party. Before then, the people were determined to abandon the party because they had realized that they were gaining nothing from it."

"So, they are back to square one. They now think their lot will be changed because they have gone back to the ruling party. Too bad. Perhaps too good. How do they see your situation - those of you on whom they had spent their lives' savings, but who completed University studies and came back to wallow in poverty with them in the villages? How do they react to their own misery itself? Is it not the water that I had to filter to wash napkins that everybody here drinks?" I asked shaking my head.

"Nobody cares about that. Our fate is that of the individual family. Most families make a mockery of us. As for their misery, you will bear witness on Sunday. It seems as if the ruling party has anesthetized the whole of Ewawa. Whatever they say is good for the country, the population accepts. That goes on and on. Politicians accuse us of fomenting rebellion in the villages. When the ruling party started losing grounds in these villages, they invited the District Officer to warn us. They tell the villagers not to listen to unsuccessful 'book people' - those of us who had returned to the villages after university studies," Jeanne expounded.

The natives took the development meeting very seriously. To them it was a showcase. To welcome their illustrious sons and daughters from cities and townships, they dressed gorgeously in oversized gowns and shirts, most probably bought when they were plump - I presume before the old man's death. The dresses were, perhaps reserved for important occasions and might have been last worn on the day of the Divisional Officer's last visit. The stains of food and wine of different occasions had left distinctive age-old marks of moulding on them. Renewed ironing with charcoal irons after a brief drying in the sun, left snail creeping-like impressions on the dresses. Some unfortunate natives had lost parts of their dresses to rats and termites and being unable to buy new ones had stitched what they had left with coarse jute bag string.

The external elite started arriving at 10 o'clock. In welcoming them, the natives genuflected, embraced and hugged their illustrious sons and daughters most tenderly. But on keen observation, one could see the alienation - the dignitaries responded as a person in white would respond to his welcoming dog trying to caress him by planting its paws on his chest. By 11 o'clock the room was full and the meeting started.

The chairman led the assembly in singing the National Anthem. After which, in his address, he thanked the Head of State for making it possible for the nine villages of the Okahmbode clan to assemble that day. He said the agreeable weather was the gift of the Head of State and prayed that God should prolong his life to further shower the clan with the customary bounties. He announced that in his magnanimity, the Head of State had appointed the son of Otang the host village, Principal of a secondary school in Dande 4. (The applause that followed was deafening.) "This is just the beginning. Politics is a bolobolo game, a give and take game. If you give me, I give you. If you don't give me, I don't give you. These nine villages can only benefit from the Head of State's development projects if they solidly rally themselves behind him. I am sure that the detractors, the rebels amongst us have heard this. And here and now, I pray that they should limit their diabolic activities within these villages. And today, today I implore all of you to denounce them once and for all. You see, the enemy is in the house. Those who could not cope with University education have returned to the villages to cause confusion. But let me warn them, the wand of justice will fall heavily on any person found disturbing the peace and tranquillity of our dear fatherland."

Although the assembly applauded, I saw the address as sterile as the speaker and what he represented. After the address, deliberations centred on the numerous problems the area was facing. The previous year's cholera epidemic and government's response were top on the agenda.

"The government reacted promptly when cholera broke out at Etambeng, Okong, and Tiata villages. A team of doctors was sent to take sample water from here. The water was then sent to France for analysis. The results came a few days ago. It is said that underground water that gives birth to springs that the people of this area drink is highly contaminated with a poisonous substance which is still to be identified. The substance increases dangerously in intensity in the dry season. That is why when we are coming here, we bring our water with us. And that is the reason why the engineers are looking for a distant water source for this area. And of course, the water source has been found. This area would have the best water system in the whole of Ewawa," the chairman boasted.

Truly speaking, all the external delegates brought mineral water with them. They even refused to wash hands with the local water during entertainment.

So long as I was concerned, there was no dangerous underground substance that contaminated underground water. The chairman was simply trying to control native anger and thus make a good political deal for himself. My friend told me later on that no doctors were ever sent to Etambeng. Furthermore, test results could not have come from France in patches.

Other discussions centred on the disadvantages of poaching, the importance of self-reliance and all that rubbish. Not a single elite mentioned the importance of building good houses in the villages. Not one talked of trying to put pressure on the government to build a dispensary at Otang. Not one elite thought of improving on the buildings of their former school, which, like all other houses around, had leaking roofs. Not one elite thought that the villages could diversify their crops and not depend entirely on cocoa and coffee. Not one elite thought of discouraging the villagers from excessive drinking. Not one elite thought that he would one day die and his remains would be brought to the village for burial, and as such, he had the obligation to press for a good water system to ease up his mourners.

So long as I was concerned, having elite like those of the Okahmbode clan, was akin to lighting a lamp and putting it under a table. Like father like son, the Okahmbode elite were husks, and if the natives relied on them for development there would be none. The elite who run away from their villages because of the fear of witchcraft, cannot improve the villages. The elite who take refuge in cities and townships alienate themselves from the villages and cannot improve the villages. And so, they should not go to the villages to ask for votes. To me the meeting was a fiasco though the natives hailed it as one of the most successful they had ever had.

According to village ethics the success of a meeting depends on how much there is to eat and drink. The elite knew that. And so they had brought assorted beers and low grade wines with them. After the meeting, they flooded the natives with them. Each village had brought prepared food to the meeting. The organizers sorted out the best and kept it in the chief's house for the elite. The villagers themselves got what remained, and shared it among the nine villages. Each village had a classroom in which to eat. Some tricksters had taken strategic positions in the chief's house while the meeting was going on. Although the Master of ceremonies tried to dislodge them to make room for the dignitaries to eat in their quiet, the fellows were defiant. They knew the elite would simply nibble at the food, and they would have the rest even if they got cudgelled in the process.

What I estimated as expenditure would have laid a solid foundation for a water project. But the natives under the guidance of their elite squandered it and left the villages without hope. To me the villages were a death trap. This conclusion was further reinforced by the mad hurry with which the elite returned to their respective towns and cities in the evening.

They had come to display position Pajeros and township speech mannerisms. That was all. They had come devoid of ideas and only left behind the empty expressions, vous voyez, vous savez, vous comprenez, n 'est ce-pas, and that acrimonious blank ululation Okahmbode Oye e! 0 ye e. Oye e! 0 ye e.

Parson, can you imagine how I felt? When there was danger in Jerusalem, Joseph and Mary fled with Jesus to Egypt. Where was I to flee now? There was danger in these villages, real health danger, danger which the elite could not identify, or if at all they did, they were not ready to tackle. Now, where was I to make my Epiphany? For two weeks, I was nervous. My stay lost its glow. I started longing to return to Dande and brace myself for the appalling decision to plead with my parents to forgive me, and take me back, or if I failed, go and plead with Joseph to re-employ me in the hotel, for me to at least take care of his son.

As I pondered over this, there was a rumour of a measles outbreak in two adjacent villages. The chiefs had appealed for help from Dande but none was forth coming. I could not remain indifferent. I had to return to Dande and hang my head in shame by doing one of the two things. I told my friend I would return in two days. She was not happy with that abrupt decision. She held me back against my will for another week, trying to get some bush meat for me.

"It is difficult to get by bush meat nowadays because conservationists comb the bushes seizing game and punishing poachers. Life has become extremely difficult. A kilo of cow meat costs 2,400 Frs. and villagers can't afford, yet they are prevented from hunting even their God-given forest animals," she remarked.

On the fourth day of the prolonged time of stay, my son developed a temperature. My heart leaped into my mouth. The temperature subsided soon after. Then it shot up in the evening and kept fluctuating at night. Before I knew what was happening, he was a full-fledged victim of measles.

We gave him village treatment. We administered enema with twenty drops of kerosene in a 'litre by eye' of water. I thought of leaving for Dande immediately to appeal to all the nooks of power to save my son. But then, the village 'nurse' who treated him told me to wait for two days before travelling with the child. She was convinced that by that time, my son would have purged out all the measles in his stomach and I would have no cause to return in fear. The next day, my son developed a terrible sore throat. He could not eat nor drink. Although my friend and her family tried to hold me back, I left for Dande.

I left in the late afternoon and so, reached Dande very late at night. Dande weather is very unpredictable in March. There was a light shower at the St. John of God Mission Quarters and moonlight at other areas. I carried my son on my back and headed for my foster-mother's house. Midway, I changed my mind and started moving toward the Holy Compound of my parents. When I got at the gate, I knocked and knocked. I knocked so violently that the Parson, further away heard the knocking and shouted that I should stop disturbing. My parents heard the knocking and asked who was there. I said I was the one. Minutes rolled by. Hours rolled by. The shower started drenching us. Finally, I decided to return to my foster-mother and ask to pass the night.

On my way, my son died. My son died on my back. My son died diee e e e e hii de hii hii hem hem hii yeh hii ... "

"Don't cry Lucia. Lucia don't cry. I now see why you are so bitter," the Parson entreated.

"Yes, Parson, my son died and I decided to give him a sailor's burial. Yes my son died and when I gave him a sailor's burial, the police came to own him. The nation came to own him. And in owning him, I became the scapegoat. And here I am, condemned to death by hanging. I am condemned to death eo, o, eo, hii, hii, hem, hem e e e e hii emmm, ... "

"Don't cry Lucia. Lucia don't cry. Don't draw me into the crying oh oooo,eh ooh oooe oh," the Parson too burst out crying.

"Don't cry yoo yooo yooo ooo, Parson don't cry," I entreated while crying.

"Lucia, my nerves are easily worked up. So, stop crying too. Take heart Lucia," the Parson entreated again.

"As you say, Parson. As you say. I am terribly worked up. I have developed a headache. My spine is throbbing with pain. I pray that we put off our story for now - after all, the story has ended. So I appeal for leave. I need a rest," I said and blew my nose.

"You are right. You really need a rest. I feel very bad at what has happened to you and I pray that we should succeed in the appeal," he concluded.

"Whether we succeed or not, I have composed a dirge for myself and I shall like you to make it part of the story.

Let them bury me in a shallow grave,

Let dogs dig it up and eat me up,
Let plunderers keep on plundering'
I've spat out Ewawa, their Ewawa
Like stale early morning spittle.

Let the truth be buried no matter how deep,
Let its grave be cemented - beton armé
Let guards keep watch with flaming swords
One day, it'll rise beyond their reach,
One day, it'll rise to be buried no more.

Let those who now eat with cooking spoons know,
The singing of the National Anthem will wither,
When the fate of Ewawa will be questioned
By the starving orphans of their creation.

Then, I shall not be the only one to hang.
Then, those who now laugh ha ha will hoot hu hu,
When the sword of real justice will have sway,
On those who plunder instead of building.

Thank God, I have now purged myself of the venom that fettered my soul. Posterity has to know that I am a victim of a tailored event and therefore not a child-killer; that our generation is a victim of a second fatiguegosimiasis; and that the avowed prisoner is the judge of Ewawian conscience.

This having been said, they can now make me rest in peace or in pieces. Amen.

Lucia Ntang

Prologue

The statement, 'Things are never what they seem', may be considered too sweeping. But Jacqueline Berke, quoting Alfred Korzybski (in Science and Sanity, 3rd ed.1948:389) celebrates the truth of it in these words, " ... the "scientific object" represents an "event," a mad dance of "electrons," which is different every instant, which never repeats itself, which is known to consist of extremely complex dynamic processes of very fine structure acted upon by and reacting upon the rest of the universe, inextricably connected with everything else ..."

Man, (ruler or subject) is a scientific object (a mad dance of electrons) that is never what it seems.

In Ewawa, and Africa as a whole, the lives of rulers slip into fatiguegosimiasis, a 'mysterious disease akin to 'aboulia' that kills them because for one reason or another, they prefer to stay in power forever. It is an incurable ailment that devastates their brains and impairs their judgement.

It attacks the frontal lobe of the brain which is the seat of judgement, reasoning, intellect and the will. The frontal lobe of the brain is responsible for spirituality and morality and therefore the seat of character and personality.

A patient of fatiguegosimiasis may not show physical abnormality. But though he may be bustling with life, he, on keen observation, shows signs of impaired morality, loss of love for the nation, loss of imagination and loss of restraint. The loss of restraint is seen in self-aggrandizement, boasting about imaginary achievements, hostility toward criticism and unfounded aggression toward intellectuals and potential rivals. The patient becomes restless, takes pleasure in travel to foreign lands, becomes manic, obsessed with foreign drinks and cigarettes, and finally becomes a victim of poor judgement. All these culminate in his making wrong choices and decisions in all domains of the politico-economic and socio-religious life of the nation. The few citizens who benefit from the blunder, become his praise singers.

The claque makes a mockery of him by dishonouring him with acts incompatible with high office. He nods approvingly in shameless ignorance. The nation weeps, he smiles.

Fatiguegosimiasis has an incubation period of five to ten years. It is full-fledged in leaders who take or remain in power at the age of seventy. It becomes schizophrenic when five to seven year terms of office are renewed several times - the curse of Africa.